FINDING FIONN

A Mystery Inspired by the Kidnapping of the Irish Racehorse Shergar

M. J. Evans

Dancing Horse Press

Foxfield, Colorado

M.J. Evans/ 7013 S. Telluride St.
Foxfield, CO 80016
www.dancinghorsepress.com

Publishers Cataloging-In-Publication Data
Name: M.J. Evans, Author
Title: Finding Fionn/M.J. Evans
Dancing Horse Press (2023) Foxfield, CO
Description: Interest: Age Level 13 and up/ Summary: It is 1983 and Ireland is struggling to survive "The Troubles." The one shining light is a champion Thoroughbred racehorse named Fionn MacCool. Irish born and bred, the horse becomes a champion and a hero for all of Ireland. But one drizzly night in February, masked men kidnap the horse from his stall. A ransom is demanded if his owner and his caregivers want to see him again. When the owner refuses to pay the ransom, his jockey, a young Irish lad named Patrick McCallin, takes it upon himself to search for his beloved horse.
Subjects: Horses, Young Adult, Mystery, Crime, Ireland, IRA, Horsemen, Racehorses, Jockeys

Library of Congress Control Number: 2023915808

Finding Fionn/ M.J. Evans -- 1st ed.
ISBN 978-1-7373618-7-9

Fionn MacCool was a central character in Irish folklore and mythology. He was the leader of the warrior band "The Fianna," known for being brave, handsome, wise, and generous.

A horse allows you to fly without wings. — *UNKNOWN*

Cast of Named Characters in Order of Appearance

Patrick McCallin – Fionn's jockey

Catherine McCallin – Patrick's mother

Sean Wiltsey - the head instructor at RACE

Ronan Boyle – Roommate at RACE

Maddie Segard– Friend at RACE from France

Mrs. Callahan – Housekeeper at Far and Away Farm

Darren Murphy – Far and Away Farm Manager

William Carroll – Irishman who wanted to purchase Far and Away Farm and all the horses, including Fionn

Sir Bran Gallagher – Trainer working for Far and Away Farm

Michael O'Reilly – Harbor Commissioner

Kylie Walsh – girl in Pub

Monsieur Martin Beaufoy – Westwind Farm owner

Madame Segard – Maddie's mother

Silas El Mari – Fionn's owner

Sir Michael Dunne – President of the Irish Thoroughbred Breeders Association

NOTE: IRA Stands for Irish Republican Army

Contents

Chapter 1

Ireland 1982

Patrick pedaled his bike as fast as his teenage legs would move. Cold, misty fog left the rough concrete of the narrow road wet and slippery. As though it were a specter appearing from the gray dawn, the stone entry to The Curragh materialized through the fog on his right. The Curragh, the most famous racetrack in Ireland and the home of five of the country's most important flat races, known as "The Classics," dated back to the Eighteenth Century. Patrick knew its history well. The first race was held there in 1866.

The Curragh was also the training facility for several stables that called the 5,000 acres of rolling Irish countryside their home.

Patrick pulled his bike over to the side of the road and laid it down in the damp grass. He hurried to the fence and, resting his chin on the top rail, waited.

His patience was soon rewarded. He felt the earth begin to vibrate. Hoof falls pounding the ground were soon followed by heavy panting. Patrick's heart beat in rhythm with the thumping. He held his breath in anticipation. Two horses burst through the fog and into view. Their nostrils flared as they sucked in the oxygen needed to fuel their bulging muscles. Tails flowed out behind them like sails in a storm. Power exuded from their bodies with each extended stride.

Riders with rounded backs perched over bent knees. Their faces were buried deep in the black manes. Their arms pumped forward and back, following the movement of the horses' heads and necks, as though they were the fulcrum around which everything else moved.

And just as quickly, they were gone, swallowed by the fog.

Patrick returned to his bike. Imagining himself mounting one of the magnificent Irish Thoroughbreds, he swung his leg over the frame.

With visions of what he had just seen repeating in his head, he rounded his back, dropped his chin to the handlebars, and raced to school.

Chapter 2

Patrick McCallin," his mother called out from the kitchen as soon as the lad stepped into the house later that afternoon. "Were ye late for school again I hear?"

Patrick lowered his blue eyes and dropped his chin. He entered the kitchen like a meek puppy, his red hair falling over his forehead. "Yeah, Ma," he said. "But only by a minit er two."

"How 'bout ten?"

"I hurried, Ma."

"Ya hurried only *after* ya watched the hearses."

Patrick had no response. He had long since learned that his mother was not one to be deceived. It seemed she always knew everything he did.

Catherine McCallin sighed in exasperation. "What am I to do with ye?" she said as she pushed an errant strand of curly red hair away from her face.

"Let me ride."

"Patrick, we been over and over this. Bein' a jockey 'tis not what I'm raisin' ye ta be. 'Tis too dangerous."

"I don't know why ye always say that. I've never heard o' anyone gettin' hurt, at least not seriously," Patrick said while he paced back and forth across the kitchen.

At just that moment, Patrick's grandfather shuffled into the room. "Lad, come with me," he said, giving his daughter a soft look of compassion. "It be time, Catherine." The old man tapped his cane and turned around, leaving Patrick no choice but to follow.

Patrick's beloved grandfather, well into his seventies, shuffled his feet as he supported his weight on his cane. He led the boy down the narrow hallway that connected the bedrooms and stopped in front of the door at the end.

Patrick knew this door opened onto a stairway leading to the attic, a place he visited only when instructed to retrieve an object of little use. He watched his white-haired, weathered grandfather open the door and slowly begin his ascent. Patrick followed, forcing himself to go as slowly as his grandfather though his young, fourteen-year-old body yearned to leap up the steps like a graceful hart.

At the top of the staircase, the old man pulled a string hanging from a single light bulb. Warm yellow light filled the attic, illuminating years of dust and cobweb-covered treasures too precious to someone, to be discarded.

Grandfather turned to the boy. "Me boy, it be time ye learned the truth."

"The truth about what, *Granda*?" Patrick asked, cocking his head to one side, and lifting his eyebrows.

"I will show ye." The old man picked his way across the rough-hewn wood planks until he reached the farthest corner where the trusses touched one another and formed a high peak to the roof. He brushed aside a thick, dust-covered cobweb and struggled to lower himself to his knees in front of an old seamen's trunk.

Patrick, curious, joined him.

"Open de trunk, lad," Grandfather said.

Patrick reached forward and pulled up on the leather handle on the front of the lid. With creaking hinges, the rounded top opened. Patrick looked inside and gasped. His eyes widened. Neatly folded, was a set of jockey silks. Made of satin, as preferred by jockeys in the cool climate of the British Isles, the body of the shirt and cap were red with a band of white diamonds across the chest of the shirt and on the front of the cap.

Patrick knotted his brows and turned to face his grandfather. "I be befuddled. Where did these come from, Granda?"

"Keep lookin', lad."

Patrick turned back to the chest. He carefully removed the silks and set them on an antique chair to his right. He turned his attention back to the contents of the old trunk. He reached in and picked up a framed picture of a man sitting on a racehorse. He was dressed in silks bearing the same band of white diamonds. The garland of roses that hung over the horse's withers and the crowd of smiling people made it obvious that this photo was taken in a Winner's Circle. Patrick brought the picture closer to his face so he could examine it more carefully. The rider looked to be quite young. His smile spread across his face, his eyes, even in the old black-and-white photo, sparkled. Patrick knew this man. He'd seen a few pictures of him throughout his childhood, but never before on a horse.

He turned to his grandfather. "This be me father? I never knew he be a jockey. Why wasn't I told?"

Grandfather nodded. "Keep lookin'."

Patrick lovingly placed the photo on top of the silks then returned to the chest. A tattered scrapbook with a green leather cover was next. He lifted it and sat back on his heels, placing the book on his lap. The brittle pages rustled as he turned them, revealing newspaper clippings and articles from racing magazines featuring the same man on various horses and wearing several different silks. With each article extolling the talents of the young jockey named Patrick McCallin, the boy's heart beat faster and his breath quickened.

He turned to the last page of the book. There, not attached to the pages themselves, was a final article. The headline screamed, "Famous Jockey Dies in Tragic Accident." With jaw clenched and tears welling up in his eyes, Patrick read his father's obituary. The final words pierced his heart as nothing ever had before: "He is survived by his wife Catherine and their newborn son, Patrick Junior."

Chapter 3

By 1982, when Patrick McCallin was just fourteen, he had lived his entire, though still short, life under the shadow of "The Troubles." Generally considered to have begun in 1968 with a series of civil rights protests, the thirty years that followed were punctuated with numerous outbursts of intense violence. The people of the Republic of Ireland where Patrick lived, Northern Ireland, and Great Britain lived daily under the fearful darkness of The Troubles. Families were torn apart, businesses were destroyed, and far too many people were killed in the violence.

And what was this all about? Patrick couldn't have told you much. It was just the way things were for him and his countrymen. Indeed, there were several issues involved of which Patrick was blissfully unaware. He had caught snatches of conversations and arguments among the townspeople, but he paid no mind to it all.

The vast majority of the island was part of the Republic of Ireland having been liberated from Britain in January 1922 after years of conflict. But a large swath of land in the northeastern corner, comprising six counties, was still a part of Great Britain. The Troubles emerged between those who felt Northern Ireland should be joined with the Republic and those who felt it should remain a part of Great Britain. Between 1922 and the outbreaks of protests in 1968, discontent was brewing.

Religion also played a part in the conflict. The Republicans in Northern Ireland were predominately Catholic. It was their desire to be united with the rest of the island republic. The Loyalists in Northern Ireland were predominately Protestant and desired to remain a part of Great Britain. Thus, the entire conflict was a scrambled mess of ideals, beliefs, and traditions. Both sides clung firmly to their principles and were willing to, and *did*, fight fiercely for what they believed.

Over the course of the conflict, numerous groups and alliances formed. The most famous and notorious of the bands of fighters was the IRA or Irish Republican Army. Even this group splintered into various factions. The largest, strongest, and most deadly of the IRA groups was called the "Provisionals." Headquartered in Belfast, this group was determined to separate themselves from British rule by any means necessary, no matter the cost in human life. They considered themselves the true IRA. They never shied away from taking credit for bombings or kidnappings of wealthy businessmen. All this was necessary, they thought, to achieve the end they desired.

Truly, it was a dark time for the people of Ireland.

Despite The Troubles, there was one thing that every Irishman could agree upon: a love and reverence for their Irish Thoroughbreds. Several breeding farms in the center of the country were producing magnificent horses, valued as racehorses in the flat races or at steeplechases, and as jumpers in the show circuit. The horses gained fame throughout Europe and America. The Irish bloodlines were much sought-after to improve the Thoroughbred and warmblood breeds. Wealthy men and women, including royalty, were investing heavily in the Irish Thoroughbred horses and breeding programs.

By a stroke of luck, Patrick found himself born into this world of Thoroughbred racing and living in the center of the racing and breeding world that pivoted around The Curragh.

Chapter 4

Now that the secret of the tragic racing accident that caused the death of Patrick's father was revealed, the boy had a clearer understanding of why his mother had been so against his desire to ride. But understanding did not mean that the yearning he felt in his bosom was any less intense. It did mean that he now had an ally in his grandfather. The old man seemed to understand that the drive within the boy could not be squelched. Patrick's grandfather set about trying to convince his daughter that Patrick should be allowed to pursue his dream.

"But I be afraid I will lose him, just as I lost me husband," Catherine whispered as she sat at the kitchen table across from her father. A tear rolled down her cheek.

"That be understandable, me dear," he said as he reached across the table and handed her his handkerchief. "But as much as we want ta, sure we can't shield the kids from every danger dat life sends der way."

Catherine looked down and shook her head. "I feel I would be sending him ta his death."

"What happened to your husband was a tragic accident . . . devastating to all of us. But it was only that — an accident. Just think how many jockeys mount up and ride the backs of those incredible animals in race after race, day in and day out. Rarely be there an accident to man or beast. It be truly the sport o' kings."

Catherine bit her lip and let another tear fall from her eye. From that moment on, Patrick's mother resolved to not stand in her son's way.

By the time Patrick turned sixteen he was old enough to enter the famous RACE program. He had spent the previous two years working as a groom, stable lad, and eventually exercise boy at one of the nearby studs.

Just down the road that connected the towns of Kildare and Newbridge, the same narrow road on which Patrick rode his bike to get to school, was the famous Racing Academy and Center of Education (RACE). It was located just fifty-four kilometers, or thirty-three miles, west of Dublin, the capital of The Republic of Ireland.

RACE was the jockey training school at the Irish National Stud near The Curragh racing and training facility. Founded in 1973, it was housed in the former home of William Hall-Walker, a man instrumental in helping the Irish Thoroughbred racehorse breeding program reach its current fame and status. The large, stately, Georgian-style home was surrounded by extensive landscaped grounds and close to the numerous training facilities in and near The Curragh. The 42-week residential program provided comprehensive instruction on race riding and horsemanship. It was Patrick's dream to enroll in the school and, with his grandfather's help, that dream came true.

When the sun rose on what would be his first day at the jockey training school, Patrick's heart was pounding, and his hands were sweating. He didn't know if he was more nervous or more excited. But either way, this was the opportunity he had always wanted, and he was going to make the most of it.

The satchel he packed a few days before was ready and sitting at the end of his bed. He looked in the mirror over the sink as he brushed his teeth. His red hair had been neatly trimmed by his mother the night before. The smattering of freckles that graced his nose and cheeks seemed to stand out, making him look even younger than his sixteen years. He scrunched his face then shrugged his shoulders. *Oh well,* he told himself, *nothing I can do about that. I'll just prove to them that I belong there. I belong on the back of a horse.*

Patrick grabbed his satchel and went to his grandfather's room. The old man spent more time in his bed these days. The lad shook the man's shoulder until the pale blue eyes opened. Focusing on his grandson, a smile stretched his dry lips. "Patrick. The day be here at last."

"I came to say goodbye and thank ye for this opportunity. I promise I will make ye proud."

"Ye always have. But I must say, it will be quiet and dull around this old house when ye be not here."

"I'll be back on the Sabbath, Granda," he said as he kissed the old man's forehead.

Patrick's mother greeted him in the hallway outside Grandfather's room, her face a puzzle of both encouragement and apprehension. Patrick said nothing as he wrapped his arms around her thin body.

Chapter 5

Patrick pedaled his bike up the long drive that led to the pale-yellow main house on the RACE grounds, the house that would be his home for most of the next year. As he biked, several cars carrying his future classmates passed him by. He pedaled faster. Soon, the lush, landscaped grounds surrounding the house came into view. Large trees framed the imposing house. A pale blue entry door was centered on the front of the house while two chimneys stood atop the roof.

Patrick parked his bike, grabbed his bag containing his belongings, and ascended the steps leading to the front door. Stepping inside, he was immediately greeted with the sounds of excited laughter. A short man in riding attire, who obviously had gained some weight over the years, came up to him.

"Welcome laddie. And you be?"

"Patrick McCallin, sir."

"Pleased to meet ye. I be Sean Wiltsey, the head instructor here at RACE," said the middle-aged man with medium brown hair and darker brown eyes, as he extended his hand.

"It be an honor to meet ye, Mr. Wiltsey. I be looking forward to learning much from ye," Patrick responded as he shook the man's hand.

"Well, there is much to learn, I must say," the older man responded with a smile. "Please go to the desk up front and get yer room assignment. Yer school uniform will be waiting for ye in yer room. Meet back down here in one hour and we will begin. No time to waste, ya know!"

Patrick found his room on the second floor. He opened the door to find another boy already dressed in the red shirt, black vest, and black breeches that all the students were required to wear.

The boy assigned to be Patrick's roommate looked up from where he sat on one of the two beds, pulling on his tall riding boots. He smiled and his eyes twinkled a welcome. "You must be me roomie."

"I be Patrick McCallin," Patrick said as he dropped his satchel on the floor.

"Pleased to meet ye. I'm Ronan Boyle. I hail from outside Belfast. Where be ye from?"

"Just down the road toward Kildare. It be so close, I rode me bike to get here."

"Aren't ye the lucky one."

Patrick nodded and smiled. "Well, I guess I best get properly dressed."

The first meeting was over lunch where the students, most of whom were boys around Patrick's age or a year or two older, received their long list of rules. This wasn't a summer camp. This was to be serious business. Not only would the students be instructed in riding, but they would also learn horse care, stable management, shoeing, saddle fitting, the use and function of various bits, horse nutrition, and much more.

A tour of the facilities and grounds followed lunch.

The main floor of the old house provided classroom space. In the basement was a gym complete with mechanical horses for practice. Mirrors lined the walls so the riders could check their position. A separate area was set aside for weight training.

Outside, the students were led across the courtyard to the yellow- and brown-trimmed stables. Stalls lined both sides of a long aisleway. Over the half-door of each stall, a lovely Thoroughbred hung his head. Each horse displayed the classic straight or slightly Roman nose, typical of the breed. A few had white stripes or stars on their faces. Some were bay, others chestnut, a few were gray. But all had dark eyes that followed the newcomers. A few horses nickered a welcome.

A covered arena was located near the stables. It was bordered by an outdoor arena, and beyond that, a narrow exercise track built in a large oval.

Patrick breathed in deeply the smell of horses, leather, and green grass as he gazed across the rolling hills toward The Curragh racecourse with its long, white grandstand. A shiver of excitement rushed through his body, and he smiled.

"Ach, would ya look at ye, grinnin' like a Cheshire cat," Ronan said, elbowing him in the ribs.

"It can't be helped. It's been ma dream come true so 'tis," said Patrick.

"Ach aye, fer me, too, lad."

Chapter 6

It took no time at all for Patrick and Ronan to become fast friends. While Patrick's goal was to become a flat-race jockey, Ronan yearned for the thrill of the steeplechase. Being that Patrick was small for his age, he was well-suited to sit the backs of the fastest Thoroughbreds, while Ronan, longer and lankier in stature, would do well to stay in the saddle over the high brush jumps and deep ditches.

But regardless of their ultimate goals, both boys attended the same classes, the same conditioning exercises in the gym, and the same riding lessons in the arena. By the end of each day of the first week, both boys collapsed on their beds feeling the same amount of exhaustion.

They started each day with fitness training, going on a three-mile run around the perimeter of the RACE complex with the other students. Patrick enjoyed these "wake-up runs," as their instructors called them, and breathed in deeply the crisp morning air. He noticed that the rain liked to take a break in the early morning, something that pleased him immensely.

After morning classes, they went to the gym for weight training and calisthenics. One warm summer day, as they were following this routine, Patrick completed his repetitions on the mat before Ronan. He stood up and went to the far side of the room where the mechanical horses awaited riders. He turned the dial to a moderate speed and set the timer for fifteen minutes. Mounting up, he pushed the start button on the artificial horse's neck. Just like the grocery store horses that start moving once a quarter is inserted, this horse's body began undulating. He stood in the stirrups and let his arms and body move with it. Glancing in the mirror to his left, he watched his form and corrected his position. He couldn't help but smile at the sight of him on the back of the black metal horse.

Suddenly, the horse began rocking violently, the rhythmic movement getting faster and faster. His body was jerked forward and back. He turned and looked over his shoulder to see Ronan clutching his stomach and buckling over, roaring with laughter.

"Turn it down! Turn it down," Patrick yelled, not the least bit amused.

Ronan, still guffawing, stood and reached up to lower the speed. "Sorry, mate," he choked out between fits of laughter. "I canna help meself."

"I not see what be so funny," said Patrick, springing off the machine.

"Then ye not look in the mirror. It be the best thing I've seen all week!"

Patrick walked past Ronan, but not until he gave him a not-so-playful punch in the gut.

On the first Sunday, and each Sabbath thereafter, Patrick and Ronan walked the short distance to Patrick's home for a warm and delicious home-cooked meal.

"Mrs. McCallin," said Ronan upon being introduced to Patrick's mother on the first visit. "'Tis a pleasure to meet ye." With his jovial personality, he greeted Patrick's grandfather just as warmly.

Grandfather and Catherine spent the entire meal quizzing the boys about their week. They wanted to know everything; no detail was to be left out. Ronan, affable as he was, kept everyone entertained as he regaled them with stories of their classes, instructors and, of course, the horses.

"And ye shoulda seen Patrick riding the buckin' bronco!" Ronan said, a twinkle in his eye.

"What?" said Mrs. McCallin, her eyes opened wide, her forehead wrinkled, as her hand flew to her chest.

"That not be funny," Patrick said. Reaching across the table and patting his mother's hand, he told the story of the trick Ronan played on him with the mechanical horse.

"On the contrary, Patrick," said his grandfather between chuckles. "me thinks that woulda been quite funny."

The meal complete, the stories told, Ronan and Patrick offered their thanks and said their goodbyes.

"I'll surely sleep well tonight," Ronan said, rubbing his stomach, "after such a delicious meal. Me thanks to ye, Mrs. McCallin."

"Until next Sabbath," Catherine said, giving both boys a tight hug.

Tired but satisfied, the two boys walked back to RACE as the pale sun was setting, sending its final rays across the waving grasses. Just as they turned up the drive leading to the old mansion, a young girl stepped out from behind a tree. Patrick stopped with a jolt.

"*Désolé*," (I'm sorry) the girl said, her accent, as well as her words, suggesting that she was from France. "I didn't mean to startle you."

Patrick recognized the girl with long, wavy black hair and large dark eyes framed by thick lashes. He had never spoken to her but had noticed her perfect form as she worked out on the mechanical horses in the gym. One of the few girls in their class, she would be hard to miss even if she wasn't so beautiful.

"Yeah, miss, ye did startle me," Patrick responded, pulling his cap from his head and twisting the rim.

Ronan punched him in the arm. "In a good way, he meant to say."

She smiled as she looked over at the sunset. With her lovely French accent, she said, "I love this time of day as the sun says, 'au revoir'." She stopped her reverie and turned to face the boys. "Forgive me for not introducing myself. I am Madeline Segard, but you can call me Maddie. And you are...?"

"P-P-Patrick," Patrick choked out. He blushed as he cleared his throat and looked down at his feet. He could feel the pull of the young woman's personality but didn't have the social skills to respond adequately.

"I be Ronan Boyle and me talkative friend here be Patrick McCallin. Pleased to meet ye."

Patrick looked over at his friend, awed at the ease with which his friend could speak to strangers . . . especially girl strangers!

She smiled. "I've been quite lonely since I left France to come to RACE. Do you have room for a new friend?"

Several months passed and the three friends strengthened their bond. Gone were Patrick's timid responses to being in her presence. In fact, he found himself looking forward to being with her. With the hard work and discipline demanded of the students at RACE, they improved their riding and horse care skills and grew in confidence. Patrick and Maddie rode together on the flat track while Ronan galloped across the grassy fields and conquered the brush jumps and ditches.

Their mealtimes and Sabbath Day dinners at Patrick's home were always spent together. Pleasant evenings found the three friends walking the grounds of the school, feeding treats to the horses, and throwing the ball for the resident cocker spaniel. Cold and windy nights were spent sitting in the comfortable living room of the old house, a fire blazing in the fireplace, an old version of the game of "Clue," called "Murder," in full swing.

"Leg up, please," Maddie said as she stood grasping the flap of her tiny racing saddle and lifting her left leg.

Patrick grabbed her leg and lifted her five-foot, ninety-eight-pound body easily. She swung her right leg over the horse's back and settled into the short stirrups. "Thanks," she said with a smile. Giving her horse a tap with the whip, she started down the track. "See you at the finish line if you can catch me," she shouted over her shoulder.

"That not be fair. Ye have a head start," Patrick called after her. She lifted her racing crop in the air in salute without turning to look at him. Patrick watched her black ponytail bounce beneath the red helmet that all the students wore, as she trotted down the dirt track. Adjusting the chin strap on his own helmet, he swung up on the seasoned gelding he would be breezing that day.

He took his horse up into a trot, standing high in the stirrups. Soon the horse picked up the canter of his own accord. Patrick looked between his gelding's ears and focused on Maddie moving gracefully on her horse ahead of them. Loosening the contact on the reins, he let his horse move out a little to catch up.

Breezing a Thoroughbred is supposed to be an easy, slow workout. But when Patrick pulled up beside Maddie, the girl gave him a crooked smile and tapped her horse with the crop. Leaping forward, both horses sensed the thrill of competition and were soon running at full speed.

The young would-be jockey got into the perfect racing form he had practiced so much on the mechanical horses in the gym. He stood slightly in the stirrups, his back rounded over his knees, his arms stretched forward, giving the gelding his head. But this was different. Yes, the mechanical horse had the correct movements, but there was an added dimension on the back of a *real* horse. There was an energy that was hard to define and impossible to measure. It wasn't something that could be turned on or off with switches and dials. This power came from deep within the magnificent animal who was allowing Patrick to join him. This ethereal element came from the heart.

Patrick's own heart quickened. He opened his mouth and focused on breathing as he stared down the track between the horse's ears. The wind blowing against his face made his eyes water. Letting go of the reins with one hand, he reached up and pulled down the goggles attached to his helmet. For over a minute, though it seemed much longer, Patrick let this once-great racehorse relive his glory days.

At the milepost, Patrick leaned back and pulled back on the reins, slowing his horse. Immediately, Maddie and her horse dashed by. The young girl smiled and waved as she and her horse darted ahead. Patrick's horse spun around, trying to be released from the hold Patrick had on him. But the jockey-in-training held tight and brought the gelding down to a controlled trot.

"There's a boy," Patrick said, soothing his eager horse. Maddie was a good twenty lengths ahead when the horse she was riding wavered and veered away from the rail. Maddie's perfect form crumpled, and she slid off the horse's left side, landing on the soft dirt of the track. She didn't move as her mount galloped down the track without her.

Patrick gasped. With eyes wide and mouth open, he watched it all unfold as if in slow motion. "Maddie!" he cried.

Chapter 7

Patrick, Ronan, and Patrick's mother walked down the hall in the hospital, stopping at room 314. The door was shut. Patrick felt his hands getting moist and his heart pounding. He twisted his hands together then looked at his mother and Ronan. Mrs. McCallin nodded, giving him the go-ahead. He raised his fist and tapped his knuckles gently on the door.

"Come in."

Though it sounded weak, Patrick knew Maddie's voice. He opened the door and entered the dimly lit room, followed by his mother and Ronan.

Standing next to the bed on which Maddie was lying was Sean Wiltsey, the head instructor at RACE.

"Mr. Wiltsey," Patrick said. "I be glad to see ye here."

"Have to take care of our girl," the horseman said, giving Maddie a pat on the hand.

"Patrick, Ronan, Mrs. McCallin, thank you for coming," Maddie said, her voice soft, her eyes puffy from crying.

Mrs. McCallin bent over and kissed Maddie on the forehead. "What can we do for ye, dear lass."

Maddie shook her head. "There's nothing anyone can do."

"What happened out there, Maddie?" Ronan asked.

"Well, I guess I might as well tell you," Maddie said, a tear rolling down her cheek. "When I was two, I was diagnosed with epilepsy."

Patrick sucked in a quick breath.

"Since my first few seizures, we found a medication that seemed to control it really well. I hadn't had a seizure for many years. We thought we had it handled." She sniffed back more tears. "We *thought* so, anyway."

Mrs. McCallin sat on the edge of her bed and took hold of one of Maddie's hands.

"Well, what are they going to do?" Patrick asked, panic rising in his chest.

"They are going to adjust the medication. It will take some experimenting, but they think they can figure it out. I guess that happens as you get older."

"But what does that mean for yer ridin'?" Patrick pressed.

Maddie sobbed.

Mr. Wiltsey stepped in to help her out. "It not be the end of the world. While she won't be able to continue training to be a jockey here at RACE, there are people with epilepsy that do ride hearses."

Patrick's mother snapped her head around and stared at the instructor. "How be that? It not be safe!"

"Well, there actually are hearses that have a 'sixth sense,' if ye will. They are intuitive enough to sense when their rider is about to have a seizure. Some hearses will just stop. Others have been known to slowly walk their rider back home. I heard of one hearse who sensed that a seizure was coming and stopped cantering and walked out of a show arena in the middle of a jump course.”

“Then we need to find Maddie one of those hearses,” said Ronan. “She canny stop ridin’.”

“So, will Maddie have to go home?” Patrick asked Mr. Wiltsey, not sure he really wanted to hear the answer.

“I have been discussin’ options with her,” Mr. Wiltsey said. “If the lass would like to finish the course, we can switch her to stable management. That certification would put her in a position to return to France in the spring and find a great job workin’ with hearses in that capacity. Then she can search for just the perfect hearse to meet her unique needs.”

Patrick looked at Maddie. “What do ye think? Will ye stay on? Ronan and I will be there to help ye with anything ye need.”

Maddie managed a weak smile.

“Ye know, Maddie,” Mr. Wiltsey said, “me thinks we might even have a hearse in the barn with the intuition I be talkin’ ‘bout. We can give him a try if ye’d like. However, a helmet will no longer be enough. We will add safety stirrups to yer saddle, and ye will always need to wear a special protective vest whenever ye are on a hearse."

Maddie pursed her lips and nodded. "I can do that," she said. "Thank you, Mr. Wiltsey."

Chapter 8

As Patrick, Ronan, and Maddie were completing their studies and training at RACE, another event was taking place just down the road toward Newbridge . . . an event that would change Patrick's life. A two-year-old colt was being trained and prepared to run his first race. Born and raised on Far and Away Farm, the young horse showed great promise, the most promise of the 1983 batch of foals the farm had produced.

Far and Away Farm was owned by an extremely wealthy businessman from the Middle East. Just two years before, he had outbid an Irishman for the purchase of the farm, and the sixty prize Thoroughbreds that went with it. Now the businessman's contact with the operation was through his on-site manager, Darren Murphy. As such, the owner rarely made an appearance in Ireland, leaving everything involving the Thoroughbred breeding, training, and racing to the manager and trainer. "All" that the wealthy owner expected was a lucrative return on his investment.

The day before Patrick and his friends were to graduate from RACE, Sean Wiltsey called the lad, now seventeen years old, into his office on the first floor of the main house.

"Ye wanted to see me, sir?" Patrick asked as he entered the office. The large room, once the home's dining room, was cluttered with books and loose papers. The dark wood-paneled walls were covered with pictures of Wiltsey's younger days as a jockey, interspersed with framed prints of paintings of steeplechases by Henry Thomas Alken. The familiar prints depicted the horses with small heads and overly long legs.

"Yeah," Wiltsey said without looking up from the paper on which he was writing.

Patrick waited.

Wiltsey signed his name on the form with a flourish then pushed the paper aside. Looking up at Patrick, he smiled. "Well, lad, ye have completed the course here at RACE, and done so with flying colors, I might add."

Patrick felt the blood rush to his face, and his freckles disappeared in a sea of red. He dipped his head and said, "Thank ye, sir. I did me best."

"Indeed. Have ye given any thought to yer next step?"

"Next step, sir?"

"Where are ye going with yer career goals?"

"I want to be a jockey, sir," Patrick responded, unsure where this line of questioning was going.

"Yeah, of course. But do ye have yer eye on any particular stable or trainer?"

"I guess I'll have to pay me dues with whomever will have me, to start."

"Perhaps I can help ye along," Wiltsey said as he smiled and winked.

"I'd be much obliged." Patrick could feel his heart beat faster.

"Far and Away Farm be just down the road. They have just hired the famous trainer Sir Bran

Gallagher. It must have taken a lot of money to get him to leave his previous post in England. But word has it that Gallagher be eager to get back to his homeland."

Wiltsey paused and gazed over Patrick's shoulder long enough for the boy to turn and look behind him. There was a large, framed picture of Sean Wiltsey aboard a bay horse, and standing beside them was the Queen of England!

Resuming, Wiltsey said, "But that is neither here nor there. Let me get right to the point. Sir Gallagher be a strong supporter of RACE. He admires the work we do here and has been impressed with our graduates. He recently contacted me. He be looking fer a young prospective jockey that he can bring along. I recommended a young lad named Patrick McCallin."

Patrick's eyes opened wide, and his face drained of blood, making his freckles stand out even more. "Me, sir? I . . . . I don't know what to say."

Wiltsey chuckled. "Ye can start by saying '*Buíochas*,' (thank you)!"

"There be no words in any language that can adequately express me appreciation."

"Well, ye have earned it, lad. Now, I'm guessing ye have stable chores to do?"

Patrick stood so quickly he knocked over his chair. "Yeah. I do, indeed," he stuttered as he righted the chair then extended his hand to Mr. Wiltsey.

Taking Patrick's hand in his firm grip, Wiltsey smiled and said, "May ye get all yer wishes but one so that ye will always have something to strive for!"

A few miles away, a large bay colt with a white blaze and four white socks, galloped around the training track.

Chapter 9

After a farewell party at the McCallin home, Maddie returned to France to look for a stable that needed a manager. Ronan went back to Northern Ireland to find a Steeplechase barn that needed a jockey. And Patrick reported for his duties at Far and Away Farm.

Far and Away Farm was located along the road to Newbridge. Its rolling acres were behind low stone walls that abutted the narrow two-lane road. It was a beautiful summer day when Patrick turned his bike up the lane marked by a carved wooden sign displaying the name of the farm.

The cold winter had delayed the arrival of the spring flowers. But now, blooms from daffodil and tulip bulbs had pushed their way up between the clumps of new grass that lined the drive, creating a welcoming atmosphere.

Patrick felt a shiver of excitement run down his spine. He smiled as he looked around while pedaling closer and closer to the farm's outbuildings. This was an enormous stroke of fortune for a beginning jockey, and he promised himself he wouldn't let it go to waste.

On both sides of the tree-lined, gravel lane were lush, green pastures. Mares with foals frolicking by their sides dotted the rolling hills. He continued pedaling up the road until white-plastered buildings with gray slate roofs came into view.

He stopped his bike and looked around. A racetrack was bordered on one side by the stables. Beyond that were more barns that housed the stallions, feed and hay, and equipment. The lane ended at a comfortable two-story house, painted to match the barns.

Leaning his bike against the side of a barn, Patrick was aware of an empty, tingling feeling in his stomach as he walked to the house. Biting his lower lip, he took a deep breath, then raised his hand and rapped his knuckles on the door.

Footsteps were heard approaching just before the heavy wooden door swung in. A plump, middle-aged woman whose red hair was braided and wrapped like a crown around her head smiled at him. "Be ye Patrick?"

"Yeah, Ma'am."

"The master has been expecting ye. Come in. Come in," she said. Her green eyes sparkled as she motioned him in. "He be in the study. Follow me, lad." As they walked down the long hallway to the side of the staircase, the woman introduced herself as Mrs. Callahan.

"I be pleased to meet ye, Mrs. Callahan."

"And I, ye," she answered as she pushed open one of the double doors on their right. Leading Patrick into the study, she said, "Master Murphy, Mr. Patrick McCallin has arrived."

Darren Murphy, the manager of Far and Away Farm and the absent owner's right-hand man, looked up from the papers he was reading. "Yeah, 'tis indeed. Welcome, lad. Sir Bran be eager fer yer arrival." He picked up the receiver on the desk phone and dialed several numbers. Waiting until someone on the other end answered, he merely said. "The lad be here." After a brief pause, he added. "I be sendin' him right along."

Leaving the main house, Patrick followed the directions to the stallion barn. He slid open the tall, heavy door and walked in, pausing a moment to let his eyes adjust to the dim light. Looking around, he took in the neat and tidy stable with tack trunks set in front of each stall and blankets folded on racks hanging from each door. Brass placards bearing the name and pedigree of each stallion were attached to the stall boards.

The back door of the barn was open, exposing the rear of a farrier's truck. Standing in the aisleway was a horse in cross-ties, the farrier, and another man Patrick assumed to be Sir Bran Gallagher.

"Excuse me, be Sir Gallagher here?"

The two men stood up and looked at Patrick.

One man stepped toward him, a smile on his face. "I be Sir Gallagher. But, please, ye can call me Bran. And ya must be me new protégé, Patrick McCallin." He extended his hand and Patrick took it. The boy felt almost giddy to be shaking the hand of this famous trainer, a man who already had been named Champion Trainer in England several times. He didn't think he could ever be comfortable calling him "Bran."

"It be an honor to meet ye, Sir...um...Bran," Patrick said, feeling his face flush.

"Ye might as well jump right in. We be puttin' aluminum racing plates on the three two-year-olds that will be makin' their debut on Saturday. These shoes be lightweight but wear out quickly. So, we put them on just a couple of days before the race. Ye hold this colt while I get Fionn."

Patrick took his post at the colt's head while Bran grabbed a halter and lead and disappeared into one of the stalls. A minute later, the trainer emerged from the stall leading a large, bay colt with a distinctive white blaze down his face and four white socks on his legs.

Hooking him up to the cross-ties, he turned to Patrick. "Meet Fionn. Ye will start as his exercise boy and groom. I want ye to get to know each other very well. He'll be runnin' in his first race on Saturday. I've entered him in the Kris Plate race at Newbury." He turned and gave the horse a pat on the neck. Smiling he added, "I have great hopes fer this one."

The moment Patrick laid eyes on Fionn, he was smitten.

Chapter 10

The next day, Patrick and Sir Gallagher, along with two stable lads and their jockey, accompanied the horses to England, two days before the scheduled race day. They ferried across St. Georges Channel and drove east to the southeast side of Newbury, West Berkshire to the famous and elegant racecourse.

The facilities at Newbury offered both flat and steeplechase races. Because of that, Patrick was on the lookout for Ronan, hoping that, perhaps, he was there with a steeplechase stable. After getting Fionn settled in his stall, Patrick started walking down each of the shed rows in search of his friend. He heard him before he saw him.

"One o' ye laddies grab a bucket fer some water. I be gettin' the hay."

"I be gettin' the water," Patrick said with a grin.

Ronan, recognizing the voice, stopped and turned around. "Well, if me eyes don't deceive me, it be Patrick McCallin. I be so glad ta see ya," he said, taking his friend in a bear hug and slapping him on the back. Stepping back, he said, "Is Far and Away running some hearses here?"

"Yeah. We brought three two-year-olds."

"Anything promisin'?"

"They all be mighty fine hearses but one . . . well, let's say he has run away with me heart."

"What be his name?"

"His name be Fionn MacCool."

Ronan chuckled. "That be a fantastic name, after the great, mythical Irish warrior."

"And he will be great, mark me words!"

It was a fine day for a horse race! The stands at the Newbury Racecourse were filled with racing fans. The turf track was fast, meaning the sod was just the right degree of firmness for the horse to grab with its hooves without becoming bogged down.

Patrick had given Fionn a bit of exercise the previous two days. The horse was in fine form, no sign of any injuries, and he galloped around the track as relaxed as if he were on a hack on the beach. Patrick groomed and tacked up the horse a short time before the man chosen by Bran to be Fionn's jockey was to mount up in the warm-up ring. Once mounted, the jockey picked up the reins. Sir Gallagher gave him last-minute instructions before the jockey tapped Fionn with his whip and trotted the beautiful horse clockwise along the white rails.

Patrick stood at the fence, watching them trot away and longed for the day he would be on Fionn's back.

"Flashy horse ye got yer eye on."

Patrick started. He turned and looked into Ronan's smiling face.

"He be a beauty, alright."

"That he be, laddie. How be his manners?"

"For a two-year-old, they be remarkable. A kind soul, that one."

The Kris Plate race was about to start, and Patrick felt his hands get sweaty and his heart start to pound. He took a deep breath, trying to calm his nerves. The field of twenty-three horses lined up at the starting pole. Patrick watched, holding a deep breath, as the race began. He watched the jockey give Fionn a tap with his crop. Fionn leaped forward, passing horse after horse. When he crossed the finish line, he had won by more than two lengths. The crowd erupted in cheers and Ronan slapped Patrick on the back.

The only other race Fionn ran as a two-year-old did not have as happy an ending. While he came in second, he lost by more than two lengths. Such is the way of the racing world.

Chapter 11

I t was a cool, winter day. Patrick was taking advantage of a break in the rain to breeze Fionn around the dirt track at Far and Away Farm. Patrick listened to the sucking sound made by his horse's feet as they pressed into and pulled up from the mud on the track. He brought the horse down to a walk and dropped the reins. Rubbing the horse's neck, he spoke softly. "That be a good lad, Fionn. Such a good lad." The winter had been good to Fionn, and he had filled out and muscled up nicely. Patrick felt confident that the horse was ready for his three-year-old season.

"Patrick, bring Fionn over here."

Startled, Patrick looked up to see Sir Gallagher standing at the gate. Gathering up his reins, he turned Fionn back and walked up to the famous trainer. Over the past several months, Bran had coached him on the three two-year-olds as they entered their third year. He was an exacting taskmaster but peppered his instructions with a generous amount of praise. Even with the pressure the trainer felt getting his charges ready for the upcoming racing season, he displayed patience and kindness with both the horses and his young exercise jockey.

"Sir Gallagher . . . er . . . Bran . . . he did great today, even with the sloppy footing."

"Yeah, that he did. And ye have a wonderful way with him. He trusts ye."

"Thank ye, Sir."

"Patrick, I have just registered Fionn for his first three-year-old race. We be takin' him to the Guardian Classic on the 20th of April. It suits me just fine if ye would be on board."

Patrick's jaw dropped. "Me, Sir?"

Bran chuckled. "Yeah. Ye be ready."

The Racing Times and the local radio sports commentators were all abuzz with the story of an unknown and inexperienced rider named Patrick McCallin, who had been chosen to ride the impressive stallion Fionn MacCool in the blue and silver silks of Far and Away Farm.

Unknown Jockey to Ride Fionn MacCool

A young man named Patrick McCallin, a graduate of RACE, has been paying his dues under the tutelage of the famous trainer, Sir Bran Gallagher. So, if the outstanding trainer, now employed by Far and Away Farm in County Kildare, Ireland, thinks the eighteen-year-old is ready, who are we to question?

Only one article mentioned Patrick's deceased father and the riding accident that killed him.

Patrick read the headlines and the articles and, as he did so, heard the voices in his head. *You can't do this. You aren't ready. Fionn deserves better.*

He threw down *The Racing Times* and paced back and forth across the room. The phone down the hall rang.

"Yeah, he be here. I be gettin' him," one of the stable lads said.

The sound of boots clomping down the hallway was heard approaching Patrick's room.

"The telly is for ye, Patrick."

Sprinting down the hall to the telephone and picking it up with clammy hands, Patrick managed to squeak out an "Yeah?"

"Patrick, it be Grandfather."

"G-Granda. Be everything all right? Ye? Mother?"

"Yeah, laddie. We couldn't be better."

Patrick licked his lips and collapsed against the wall.

"I just wanted to call and tell ye how proud we—both of us—be of ye. As ye ride that hearse today, know that yer pa will be right there watchin' over ye."

The moment Bran lifted him into the saddle, Patrick's butterflies fluttered away. A sense of calm swept through him, and he gathered up the reins with an air of confidence.

"Don't ye worry 'bout stickin' to the rail," Bran coached. "Just find the clearest path and let the hearse run his own race."

Patrick nodded.

"And lad," the sage trainer continued, "stay in the saddle."

Patrick smiled and waved his whip.

Fionn's ears twitched back and forth as they paraded past the judges' stand and the grandstand. Cameras flashed and the crowd roared its approval as Patrick steered his mount toward the barrier gates marking the starting line.

Fionn plunged into the narrow stall with metal walls that separated the horses. Patrick took a deep breath and let it out slowly, rubbing Fionn's neck as they waited for the barrier to be lifted. Almost at once, the gates sprung open, and they were off.

Fionn fought for his head as Patrick pulled at the bit. Then, the inexperienced jockey remembered Sir Gallagher's instruction: "Let the hearse run his own race."

The race was run in a clockwise direction over sod. Fionn ran most of the race along the rail near the front but when the field rounded the last turn, Fionn decided he had enough of the crowded conditions. With two furlongs left to the race, the horse took over, blazing ahead and winning the race by seven lengths.

Passing the finish post, Patrick stood in his stirrups and looked back over his shoulder. In shock, he realized just how spectacularly they had won. He shook his whip in the air and let out a whoop.

For the first time in his life, Patrick found himself in the Winner's Circle, with crowds of people all trying to talk to him at once. And for the first time in his life, Patrick was at a loss for words.

With such a spectacular showing, Fionn and Patrick were now the favorites to win the most important race of the season, The Epsom Derby.

Chapter 12

For more than two centuries, The Epsom Derby has been the defining test of a Thoroughbred. The Derby is run over a distance of one mile, four furlongs, and ten yards on an undulating course with a sod surface. The Derby remains one of the most prestigious races in all of Britain. The race is held on the first Saturday in June at Epsom Downs in Surrey, England. It is open to three-year-old colts and fillies.

As it was one of the most important races in England, thousands of people crowded into the stands and infield on this bright sunny day to catch a glimpse of the finest three-year-old racehorses of the year. After Fionn's showy victory in his previous race, the flashy colt was the easy favorite to win this year's race. The name on everyone's tongue was "Fionn."

Patrick, preferring to act as Fionn's groom as well as his jockey, was at the shed row where Fionn was stabled well before sunrise the morning of the race. Seeing the other grooms and stable lads bustling about actually served to distract him from the upcoming race and settle his nerves.

Fionn calmly munched his hay while Patrick mucked his stall. As he worked, Patrick rehearsed in his mind all the instructions he was previously given by Bran. The odd configuration of the track – set up in a horseshoe shape – made for some careful planning. Fionn and Patrick were to come out of the final bend, called Tattenham Corner, pick up speed, and sail down the incline to the finish line in front of everyone else . . . if all went according to plan.

Patrick brushed his red curls off his face and wiped the perspiration from his neck. This was an exciting day, but one not without its risks. The headline announcing the death of his father flashed through his mind. He shook his head to dislodge the image. "We can do this," he said to Fionn. Fionn never seemed to question it as he gave Patrick a nudge with his muzzle.

Once again, Sir Gallagher lifted Patrick up in the saddle. Once again, he said, "Let Fionn run his own race." The trainer gave Patrick a slap on his boot and Patrick and Fionn stepped onto the soft, green turf.

It was mid-afternoon when The Epsom Derby entrants entered the track. Fionn loaded into the gate without an issue, almost as though he wanted to shrug his shoulders and say, "This again?"

The race started smoothly, and Fionn broke from the gate on stride. Patrick relaxed his arms and let them follow the pumping of Fionn's neck and head as the pair started up the first hill, safely in the middle of the large mass of charging horseflesh and shouting humans. The footing was good and Fionn was having no trouble stretching out and picking up speed, secure in the rhythm he had established. Patrick willed himself to be calm, almost motionless.

Fionn found a comfortable spot in fourth place on the outside as they started down the first hill. Patrick looked straight ahead at the three horses in front of them as tears from his watering eyes rolled down his face. Going up the next hill at the three-quarter mark, Fionn was about four lengths behind. Patrick kept him a few horses back for most of the race, but once they reached Tattenham Corner, he lifted his right hand and gave Fionn a tap with the crop. Fionn, as though insulted, burst forward. Patrick felt the horse veritably explode beneath him.

Down the last hill and around the final corner, Fionn appeared to have the race won already in his own mind. Nothing was going to stop him. The horse knew what he was meant to do. Calm and confident, the Thoroughbred ran with his tongue lolling out the side of his mouth.

Fionn moved up to third, then second, and then, in the blink of an eye, was in the front of the pack. Nothing was ahead of them but the long, downhill stretch of green turf, leading to the finish line.

Fionn won the race by the biggest margin ever seen at The Epsom Derby, almost ten lengths ahead of the next horse. Fionn and Patrick were so far ahead, the second-place jockey, not seeing anyone in front of him, thought *he* had won! It was one of the most memorable moments in horse racing history.

A cheer went up from thousands of throats. Hats were tossed in the air. Everyone knew they had just witnessed history in the making.

With a smile across his face, Patrick's heart pounded as he was led to the Winner's Circle. Fionn's coat glistened with sweat as camera bulbs flashed in the horse's face.

Patrick sat atop Fionn; his heart filled with a joy he had never felt before. He turned his face toward the sky, letting the sunshine wash over him. Closing his eyes, he thought of his father and hoped he was looking down on him at this very moment. *Have I made ye proud of yer son?* He thought. A tear squeezed out of the corner of one eye.

Sir Gallagher pulled the young jockey down from the saddle and enveloped him in a tight hug. It was the thing dreams are made of.

Years later, Patrick would still look back at giving Fionn the whip with regret. "Fionn knew how to win," he said in an interview. "All I needed to do was steer. He didn't need the whip. Didn't deserve the whip."

But on this day, all he could do was revel in the glory and excitement of being in the Winner's Circle with the kind of horse every jockey hopes to have the chance to ride.

Fionn and his performance at The Epsom Derby became the talk of not only the horse racing crowd but also the subject of conversation in every pub in Ireland. Their home-grown stallion was showing the rest of the world what he was made of and putting Ireland and its Thoroughbred breeders on the map.

Two weeks later, at the beginning of May, Fionn ran away from the fairly mediocre field in the Chester Vase, a length of one mile, four furlongs, and sixty-three extra yards for good measure. Held in Chester, England at one of the oldest facilities in the country, the race was run over a nearly circular course. The horses ran to the left on a turf track.

Winning by twelve lengths, Fionn treated it like a Sunday walk in the park. The crowds loved it!

Chapter 13

While Patrick and Fionn were in England, bringing fame and fortune to the absent owner of Far and Away Farm, the Irishman, William Carroll from Dublin, who lost the bidding for the farm and its horses to a foreigner, was not making a secret of his displeasure. "Far and Away Farm and its horses are Irish and should be owned by an Irishman," he would tell anyone who would listen. Some people agreed. Others shrugged their shoulders and were just pleased with the attention Fionn was bringing to all of Ireland's horses.

But that was a minor conflict compared to the other issues the Irish had to deal with. The Troubles in Ireland were in full swing. It seemed the warmer weather had brought out the worst on both sides.

Belfast was a war zone and looked like it. Numerous bombings left several of the cafés and stores in tatters. People were afraid to go to town. Businesses boarded up their windows and doors and shut down.

But running a war was an expensive venture, especially the way the IRA Provisionals were doing it. Guns and ammunition were expensive. Bomb-making supplies didn't come cheap, either. While some of the "Provos" came from comfortable backgrounds, others found running a war cut into their daily living expenses. Money was needed.

The short-lived DeLorean Motor Company operated in Dunmurry, just outside Belfast, from 1978 until the company went bankrupt in 1982. It had produced nine thousand of the sporty and uniquely designed DeLorean sports cars, and lots of jobs for the locals. With its demise, hundreds of men were without jobs. Many of those carried their anger into the ranks of the IRA.

In mid-May, while Fionn was preparing for The Epsom Derby in England, two black Renaults moved slowly up a tree-lined street in Dublin. The homes bordering the street were large, and a particularly opulent one belonged to a former high-level executive from the DeLorean Motor Company, now maintaining his wealth in the export business. The cars moved to the curb in front of that mansion. The massive home was surrounded by a decorative wrought-iron fence. The driveway was blocked by an equally ornate gate. A light was seen shining in one of the upstairs windows. A porch light lit the entry. The men in the Renaults turned off their engines and waited.

An hour later, a DeLorean pulled up to the gate and stopped. The driver, a man in his fifties, stepped out of the car and walked casually up to the gate as he pulled a key from his pocket. He turned the key in the lock, pushed open the gates, and pivoted around to return to the vehicle. As he did so, he was ambushed from the side by two men wearing only black. The men pushed the driver to the ground and held him there at gunpoint. The terrified driver put up his hands and cried, "Don't shoot. Don't shoot!"

"Shut up," growled one of the men.

A young man sitting in the passenger seat of the DeLorean gasped. "Hey! What be going on out there?"

He had no time to react before a third assailant leaped into the driver's seat, closed the winged door, put the car in reverse, and squealed around in the street, driving away with a roar of the engine.

The driver, the victim of the attack at the gate, was dragged into the front garden of the mansion and dumped in a flower bed. His two attackers left him groaning in pain as they ran back to the Renaults, started their engines, and did their best to keep up with the DeLorean.

If this had just been a carjacking, few people would have cared, including the Garda, the local police. But seated in the passenger side of the sports car was the executive's twenty-year-old son. That made it a kidnapping and a different story entirely.

A half-hour later, the DeLorean spun around a corner in an old part of town and entered an abandoned warehouse through a garage door. The Renaults limped along behind but eventually joined it. The garage door came down with a bang, sealing off the entrance.

The kidnapping victim, frozen in fear, offered little resistance as he was blindfolded by his captors and taken to a musty room that had once been an office. He was locked inside and left alone to worry about his future.

The driver, who had been attacked at the gate, managed to struggle on his hands and knees to the front door of the mansion. He lifted his hand and pounded the palm against the bell before collapsing on the front stoop. When the door was opened by a member of the household staff, the poor man was found unconscious in a heap on the step. It was several hours later before he was finally awake enough to offer any information.

The demand for **one million pounds, to be paid in hundred-pound notes, came to the mansion by way of a phone call early the next morning. The wealthy executive took the call and immediately agreed to pay the ransom. Arrangements were** quickly made for how and where the money was to be paid, and the executive's son was released the next day.

The IRA took credit for the kidnapping with a letter to the local newspapers. A lucrative source of income was now available to the rebels.

Chapter 14

Fionn's fourth race was back in his own neighborhood. The horse was allowed a glorious homecoming by being entered in the Irish Derby, held at The Curragh. He easily became one of only thirteen horses to win both The Epsom Derby and The Irish Derby. Winning by four lengths, it appeared as though the horse was not even breathing hard.

A splendid parade was held in Fionn's honor down the main street of Newbridge. Patrick led the prancing stallion as the townsfolk cheered. Fionn, his head and tail up, pricked his ears and looked from side to side. His eyes were open so wide one could see white all around the dark brown iris.

Seeing Fionn's nerves on edge made Patrick chuckle. "Ye can run with the best and leave them in the dust, but a little parade through the village scares ye."

Children ran into the street to give Fionn carrots and apples. Parents ran into the street to capture their children.

Fionn had become a national hero, a bright spot in the lives of every Irishman, a people whose lives were otherwise filled with such darkness and destruction.

Fionn's Middle Eastern owner decided to let Fionn retire in a blaze of glory. In the horse racing world, the real money is not made from winning races but in renting the horse out for breeding. The race victories just prove the horse's value and desirability as a stud. Thus, Fionn returned to his home at Far and Away Farm a national hero, the European Horse of the Year, and a much sought-after stallion for breeding to the best mares.

A shiny brass plaque was attached to his stall door. It read:

FIONN MACCOOL - HORSE OF THE YEAR

Chapter 15

While Fionn's career as a racehorse had ended before he even turned four, Patrick had his whole life ahead of him. Sir Gallagher kept Patrick busy throughout the winter, training the new crop of two-year-olds and getting the three-year-olds ready for their next year of racing.

The daily routine involved feeding horses, mucking stalls, taking horses to the fields for turn-out, and breezing the horses getting trained to race. It was hard work, but Patrick enjoyed it.

One misty, gray morning, Patrick stepped out of the barn, intent on returning to the main house to make a sandwich. He stopped and looked around at the rolling green hills, divided by hedgerows and stone walls. He breathed in deeply the crisp country air as he listened to the warbling birds in the brush and the occasional whinny of a horse. He was filled with joy at being home in Ireland after the English race season. He truly loved Ireland, even with all its troubles. Yes, he admired England, envied it in some ways, but it was Ireland that he loved down to his marrow. He fairly skipped all the way to the house, a smile across his face.

Once his work and assignments were completed, Patrick was free to spend time with Fionn. He loved the rain on his face as he trotted the stallion over the grassy hills of the farm and down the quiet road. He breathed in the smell of the coming winter as Fionn's hooves crushed the fallen leaves.

Upon returning one afternoon, Patrick and Fionn approached the stone entry to Far and Away Farm to find workmen installing a sturdy gate between the entry pillars. The workmen waved him through, and he rode up the lane beneath the leafless trees. Back at the barn, he found Bran.

"They be puttin' up gates, I see," he said to Bran as he rubbed Fionn's coat to get it dry.

"Yeah," Sir Gallagher said, his hand stuffed in his pockets. "With all the Troubles in Ireland, I felt we needed to beef up security at the farm."

Patrick stopped rubbing his horse and tossed the damp towel over his shoulder. He turned to face his trainer. "Do ye think we be in danger?"

"Perhaps not us. It be the hearses I fear for."

Patrick caught his breath. "The hearses?"

"Fionn in particular."

Patrick clutched Fionn's halter. "What mean ye?"

"In case ye didn't realize it, Fionn is worth millions o' pounds." Sir Gallagher removed his hands from his pockets and rubbed his temples. "I been tryin' ta get Murphy to beef up security. I tried to get cameras installed in the barns, but he said the £1,000 price tag was too much. £1,000? How can that be too much when we have hearses like Fionn worth millions!" Sir Gallagher's face was getting redder and redder with each word. He threw up his hands in surrender. "The gate was all I could get, and even that won't be locked."

"What about the owner? Be he concerned?"

"It don't appear so. I guess The Troubles in Ireland don't affect him much while he sails his yacht 'round the Mediterranean." The disdain was not lost on Patrick.

Bran turned on his heels and marched down the aisle. "Let's just pray our beautiful charges be safe," he said over his shoulder. He stopped and turned back toward Patrick. "Oh, one more thing. The first of the mares for Fionn be arrivin' next week."

With spring in the air, Patrick and Sir Gallagher took several two- and three-year-olds to England for the racing season. Fionn was left behind to pursue his career as a stud and the father of the next generation of racing champions.

Fionn's first year as a stud was quite successful. He covered thirty-five of the finest mares from around Europe, all but one of whom conceived.

His absent owner purchased a new yacht.

While Fionn was doing his job at Far and Away Farm in Ireland, Patrick was keeping busy riding fast Thoroughbreds in the races in England. After winning The Epsom Derby, he was in great demand as a jockey. He rode horses in all the big races, both horses trained by Sir Gallagher as well as fillies and colts run by other trainers. His reputation as an excellent jockey was spreading far and wide.

By the end of the season, Patrick and Sir Gallagher returned with their horses to Far and Away Farm. They knew the winter would be busy keeping their horses in shape and training a new crop of two-year-olds. Sometimes, Patrick had to pinch himself to make sure the life he was living wasn't just a dream.

The best part of returning home was being reunited with Fionn. Their relationship was as close as ever, even with Patrick's long absence.

"Don't worry, Fionn," he said, giving the horse a carrot and rubbing his blaze. "Ye be still the best there be."

One evening, shortly before the Christmas holiday, he received a call from William Carroll, the businessman from Dublin who had attempted to purchase Far and Away Farm and all its horses.

"Lad, this be William Carroll," the man said, his tone abrupt and business-like.

"Good evening, sir," Patrick responded, trying to conceal his surprise. He knew of the man, of course, but had never spoken to him.

"I be a busy man, so I will get right to the point," Carroll said. "I be plannin' to expand me interest in hearseracing. I be goin' ta start a new breeding facility, and I would like ta have a full-time jockey on me staff to run me up-and-comin' hearses. I would like ye to be that person."

"Uh . . . sir . . .," Patrick stammered.

"Yeah, yeah, I know this be a surprise, but I am prepared to double whatever salary ye be paid by that foreigner who stole Far and Away Farm out from under me."

Patrick cleared his throat. His head was spinning, and he blinked his eyes to gain his bearings. He knew immediately what he wanted to do. "I thank ye, sir, for the generous offer. But, for the time being, I plan ta stay workin' fer Sir Gallagher. If the occasion arises where I don't have a mount, I would be happy ta step in and help ye."

"No dats not what I want atol," Carroll said, irritation rising in his voice. "I want all the rights to a full-time jockey er not atol."

The phone went dead.

Patrick moved the buzzing phone away from his ear and stared at it, his brows knitted. *That be certainly unexpected,* he thought.

Chapter 16

ebruary was cold and damp, perhaps more so than typical. Patrick put on a warm coat and went about his chores.

Fionn nudged Patrick as his favorite lad led him back to his stall from the pasture. It was dinnertime, and the stallion was clearly impatient as he pushed Patrick forward.

Patrick chuckled and rubbed Fionn's white blaze, musing, "You'd think I never fed ye."

The young jockey was glad for the winter break from the hectic racing schedule the rest of the year. The racing season was on hiatus and the breeding season had not yet begun. January and

February were not only a rest for the horses but for the riders, as well. The surprising call from William Carroll had been all but forgotten as Patrick and Sir Gallagher worked with the horses in training.

On this day, Sir Gallagher was out of town, and Patrick was eager to get home for a warm meal. He hurried through his chores, feeding and blanketing Fionn, fluffing up his straw, and giving him a carrot. Convinced that all was well, he left the stable lights on, knowing Murphy would do a final check around eight-thirty. He stepped outside into the chilly, foggy night. The small, skinny lad shivered from the cold. He screwed down his cap and buttoned up his coat before mounting his bike, then rode down the lane beneath the naked trees.

Approaching the gate, he got off his bike, pushed open the gate, and walked his bike through. After latching the gates back together, he hopped on his bike and headed for home. A few meters down the road, he swerved around an old, beat-up black Volkswagen that was parked on the shoulder of the road. He almost hit it, not seeing the car through the fog before he was nearly upon it. As he passed by, he glanced at the dark window of the driver's door. All he could see inside was the silhouette of two men and the orange glow from a cigarette. Turning back to face the front, he looked over his handlebars and pedaled home.

Odd as it was to have a car parked along the road, he paid it no mind as he continued down the road. Still not concerned, he entered his home and greeted his mother and grandfather.

Darren Murphy and his family lived in the farmhouse on the Far and Away property. As such, it was his job to do the night check of all the horses before retiring each day. He walked up and down the aisles, rubbing a nose here, running his fingers through a forelock there. Entering the stallion barn, he peered into Fionn's stall. The big, bay horse was sleeping soundly on his side and didn't even open an eye.

Murphy clenched his jaw as he headed toward the door. He paused at the light switch that controlled the overhead lights. Breathing out a sigh, he left the lights on and walked out the door.

Shortly after Murphy returned home, a Ford Granada pulling a two-horse trailer drove down the main road that connected the towns of Kildare and Newbridge. Its headlights were off. In the fog, it was nearly impossible to see. As the car with the trailer neared the entrance to Far and Away Farm, the driver of the Volkswagen, which had been sitting on the side of the road for several hours, started its engine, pulled the vehicle around, and followed the horsebox.

When the lead car pulled up to the gate, the driver slammed on the brakes.

"I didn't think there would be a gate," said the driver, irritation in his voice.

"Don't worry. It not be locked," said a man sitting in the passenger seat dressed in a Garda uniform. He leaped out of the Granada, approached the gate, and released the latch. He pushed the two gates open and got back in the car.

"See. Me source be correct," he said as he closed the passenger door on the Granada. "It not be locked."

The Granada pulling the trailer lumbered through the opening. The Volkswagen followed.

Both cars slowly moved forward in the darkness and drove up to the house. The only sound was the crunching of the tires on the gravel lane.

"He told us to go to the house first, and the man who oversees the farm will show us which hearse," said the man who had opened the gate. "Let's get the man, load the beast, and get out o' here."

"Grab yer gun."

The passenger stopped halfway out the door. Looking back, he snarled, "Nobody gets hurt. Do ye hear me!"

"Just props, just props."

"See that they stay that way."

Two men from the Volkswagen also climbed out of their car. They, too, were dressed in black. Masks and scarves covered their faces. In their hands, they also held guns.

Inside the house, the Murphy family was preparing for bed. The four children were taking turns in the bath while Mrs. Murphy made sure they came out clean. Mr. Murphy was in his study, a fire crackling in the firebox, a small lamp lighting the papers on which he was writing.

A loud pounding on the front door interrupted the peaceful evening. Murphy's oldest son, newly dressed in night clothes, ran to the door. He opened it to see a man dressed in the uniform of the Garda, the local police.

"We be here to see Mr. Murphy," the stranger said as he pushed his way into the house and past the frightened boy.

Murphy, hearing the ruckus in the hallway came out of his study. "What's goin' on here?" he said, his voice shaking as four masked men, three of whom were armed, stormed into the house.

"Gather yer family," ordered the one dressed in the Garda uniform.

"Please don't hurt us," Murphy pleaded. "Take whatever ye want, but don't hurt me family."

"If ye cooperate, no one will get hurt."

The men herded Mrs. Murphy and the four children into the study. They ordered them to sit together on the floor. Mrs. Murphy wrapped her arms around the children and glared at the men.

Two men stayed in the house, guarding the family, while two others pushed Mr. Murphy out the door, grabbing his coat on the way out. "Here," said one while tossing it to Murphy. "Ye be needing this."

Noticing the horsebox in the drive, Murphy looked at the men. "Ye came for the hearse. So where be ye takin' me? And why be ye threatenin' me family?"

"Just get us to the hearse. We be dealin' with ye as we see fit."

The lights in the stallion barn were glowing through the fog, turning the mist that hung in the air a pale yellow. With the lights still on, the stallion barn appeared as a beacon in the night. Murphy led the men down the lane toward the stables. Entering the barn, several horses put their heads over the stall doors. Some nickered a greeting. One of those was the friendly Fionn.

"Wait here," Darren Murphy said to the two masked and armed men who accompanied him. Murphy walked directly to Fionn's stall. A brass plaque with his name and "Horse of the Year" title was attached to the stall door. He lifted a leather head collar and lead from the hook beside the stall and placed it on Fionn, attaching the hook under the stallion's jaw. Murphy struggled to keep his hands from shaking and his breathing slow and calm. While horses can sense danger, Fionn showed no concern, having developed trust in the barn manager.

"Be that the right hearse?" the taller of the two men said.

"That be the one," replied the man in the Garda uniform. "I recognize him from his picture."

"All hearses look alike to me."

"This be Fionn," Murphy assured them. "What are yer goin' to do with him?"

"Ye take him and load him up in the trailer," said the tall man.

"Only if ye guarantee that nothin' will happen to ma family," Murphy said, perspiration beading on his forehead.

"Ye do what we say, and nothin' will happen ta them."

Murphy took a deep breath and concentrated on calming his pounding heart. He led Fionn out of the barn and into the dark night. The Thoroughbred tossed his head in confusion but otherwise followed along obediently. As they approached the horsebox, Fionn stopped, his ears twitching forward and back.

"Walk forward, Fionn," said Murphy, giving a slight tug on the lead. "Be a good lad now."

Fionn snorted.

"Ye be fine. These men will take good care of ye." Murphy glared at the kidnappers and added, "Be sure that ye do. Do either of ye know how to take care of a high-spirited hearse like this?"

"That be no concern of yer's," said the man in the Garda uniform. "Just get the beast in the lorry if ye want to see yer family again."

Murphy struggled to keep himself calm for Fionn's sake. "Load up, Fionn, load up," he said as he walked straight up the ramp ahead of the horse. He expertly guided Fionn into one of the straight-load tie stalls while he walked to the front of the box in the other stall. He clipped the trailer tie to the head collar and unclipped the lead. Walking out of the horsebox, he shoved the lead at the chest of the man in the Garda uniform.

"When ye unload him, make sure ye back him out slowly and straight down the ramp. I not want him gettin' hurt," he said as the kidnappers closed the double doors and lifted the ramp to the horsebox.

The taller man got into the Granada alone, started the engine, and drove down the lane. The car and trailer soon disappeared into the foggy night. A soft rain started falling, mixing with the tears that rolled down Murphy's cheeks.

Chapter 17

Get movin'. We ain't got all night," the remaining man, the one dressed in the Garda uniform, said as he shoved Murphy down the lane toward the house.

"I want to go back to me family," Murphy said, his fists clenched. One on one he felt he could handle the guy, but there was the safety of his family to consider.

"You'll be comin' with us fer a bit. Cooperate and nothin' will happen to ye or yer family."

"Comin' with ye? What be that about?"

"We want to make sure ye don't contact the Garda."

"I won't. I promise. Just let me return to me family. They must be so frightened. This wasn't supposed to go down like this." Murphy stopped in the middle of the lane and glared at the man. His heart was racing. A shiver went down his spine.

"Just get in the car," the kidnapper said, shoving him in the tiny back seat of the little car while the two remaining men ran out the front door of the farmhouse and climbed in the front.

For the next two hours, Murphy was driven around the countryside, mainly on back roads, until he was so confused that he had no idea where he was. The men said nothing, just kept driving. As they drove through the night, Murphy saw no sign of the horse trailer carrying Fionn. It was clear they weren't following it.

Sometime after midnight, the car pulled to the side of the road.

"Ye be gettin' out here," said the man in the Garda uniform.

Murphy pulled open the door and felt the man shove him from behind. He tumbled out, landing in the weeds as the car's tires spun in the loose gravel before connecting with the pavement and zooming off.

Murphy pushed himself to his feet. His first thought was gratitude that he was alive. His second thought was, *Where am I?* In the dark and the fog, he had no way of knowing which way to turn. Pulling his jacket tightly around him, he made a guess and started walking.

The night grew colder, and the rain started coming down faster. Murphy increased his pace as he searched for a house whose inhabitants might help him. At last, he saw a yellow light glowing from the window of a small home set close to the road. He opened the rickety gate and walked up the weed-strewn path to the door. Tapping lightly, he waited. A minute later, a man, balding and wrinkled, opened the door a crack.

"Ye want somethin'?"

"Please, sir. I be kidnapped and set free a far piece down the road. I be walkin', searchin' for help," Murphy said as he rung his hands. With pleading eyes, he added, "I don't know where I be. Might I please use yer telly to call me brother to come get me and take me home?"

The old man paused while his eyes searched Murphy from head to toe. "Ye seem harmless enough," he finally said. "Come in, but don't wake the missus. She don't take kindly to strangers."

Murphy arrived home in the wee hours of the morning just as the clock on the living room wall was striking three. He burst in the door and called out to his wife. A cry was heard from his office. He rushed into the room to find his wife and four children sitting on the floor, tied together. The two youngest children were slumped over, sleeping. His wife and the two oldest were crying.

Murphy knelt beside them and began untying the ropes that held them bound.

"Be everyone okay? Be any of ye hurt?"

"I have to go to the bathroom," sniffled the youngest as she rubbed her eyes.

Pulling the last rope away, he lifted the child, "Off with ye then," Murphy said.

"Where have ye been?" his wife asked, wiping the tears from her children's faces.

"The kidnappers drove me out in the country and dropped me off to find me way home."

"Did they take Fionn?" asked Mrs. Murphy.

Murphy dropped his eyes and nodded.

"Is he going to be okay?"

"I was promised that he would be well cared-for."

"I'm not sure we can trust them. Let's call the Garda."

"No!" exclaimed Murphy. "They threatened to come back and hurt us if we did."

"Then what can we do?"

"I be going to call Sir Gallagher. I'll let him take care of it from here. Sure I don't want ta be involved atol or risk me family."

Chapter 18

Sir Bran Gallagher was awakened at 4:00 a.m. when the phone in the hall began ringing. He rolled over and covered his head with his pillow, hoping it would stop. It didn't.

Pushing back his quilt he sat up and slipped his feet into his house shoes. With a deep sigh of resignation, he stood and walked down the hall. Picking up the receiver, he heard:

"Fionn be gone."

Suddenly, Sir Gallagher was wide awake! "What do ye mean, 'He be gone'?"

"Kidnapped. Stolen."

"I be right there." Gallagher slammed down the phone and ran to his room to get dressed.

Less than five minutes later, he was in his car, driving toward Far and Away Farm.

Gallagher's little BMW swerved into the entrance at Far and Away Farm, sending gravel splaying behind it. He roared up the lane and skidded to a stop at the stallion barn. He had to see for himself, still convinced that there must be some mistake. The lights were on in the barn, and he pushed open the door.

His heart dropped as he looked into Fionn's empty stall. He rubbed his temples, wishing this was all a bad dream. Fionn, the wonderful, prize stallion of the farm was truly gone. He clenched his teeth, spun around, and drove the short distance to the farmhouse.

Patrick McCallin knew something was wrong the minute he turned onto the lane leading to Far and Away Farm. The fields were too empty. The barns were too quiet. He started pedaling as fast as his heart was beating. He noticed Sir Gallagher's car parked in front of the farmhouse – another sign that something was wrong. The trainer spent all his time in the stables. Patrick kept going to the stallion barn.

Fionn's stall door was open, but the stallion was nowhere to be seen. Patrick checked every stall. He ran outside and gazed over the paddock fence toward Fionn's pasture. There was no sign of the big, bay stallion with the white blaze down his face.

The young jockey's heart was pounding in his throat and his stomach was turning as he ran to the mare barn. Inside, a groom was pushing a cart of feed from stall to stall. Frantic, Patrick grabbed the lad from behind and spun him around. "Fionn! Where be Fionn?"

The lad, wide-eyed with fear, shook his head.

Patrick ran out the door and up to the farmhouse. He burst through the door without knocking. "What's happened to Fionn?" he cried out, his voice shaking.

At that moment, the ringing siren from a Garda vehicle was heard in the distance. It grew louder and louder.

Sir Gallagher pushed past him and went outside to greet the police.

Patrick stepped to one side, watching and waiting. He felt his body heat rising and a twisting in his stomach.

Sir Gallagher returned with two Garda officers. He took them into the study. Patrick, though uninvited, followed.

"Approximately what time was the hearse taken?" one of the officers asked.

Taken? Patrick collapsed into a wingback chair. He listened in stunned disbelief as Sir Gallagher explained the situation.

"Mr. Murphy said he be ordered ta load the hearse into the lorry at 'bout nine p.m."

Both policemen shook their heads. "Ye mean to say the kidnappers have a ten-hour head start on us?" said the taller and heavier of the two men. "They could be anywhere in the Republic or the North."

"Why didn't ye report this earlier?" asked the other, a short, red-haired man.

"Mr. Murphy was taken away at the same time and not released until well after midnight. It took him several hours ta find his way home. He called me at 4 a.m. At that point, I came directly here to verify that the hearse be indeed gone. I then spent a couple of hours trying ta reach the hearse's owner. Only then did I have permission to contact ye."

"Well, if it's a kidnapping, or should I say, a hearse-napping, there will be a ransom demand," said the short officer. "Have ye been contacted?"

"No."

"Well, it shouldn't be long before we hear somethin'. Dat's how these things work."

While Bran paced, the Garda sent officers to set up checkpoints on the main roads. They were looking for a Granada pulling a heavy, two-horse trailer. While numerous horseboxes were out and about, one being pulled by a Granada should be easy to spot.

The call came in at 9 a.m. Gallagher took it. The Garda stood beside him, listening.

"Be this someone in charge of Far and Away Farm?" said the muffled voice on the other end of the line.

"To whom be I speakin'?"

"That be no concern of yers. Suffice it to say, I be here with the hearse."

"Be Fionn safe?"

"At the moment he be. But that can change at any time."

"I want Fionn back, uninjured. I assume ya want us ta pay a ransom."

"If ye want to see the hearse again."

"How much is the demand?"

"Ye will need ta pay two million pounds."

Gallagher gasped. "T-two million pounds?" The trainer wiped his forehead with his handkerchief. "That not be easy. It be goin' ta take some doin'. I'll have ta talk with his owner."

"See that ye do. I be callin' back in twenty-four hours."

'I'll do me best, but ye have ta understand these things take time."

"Ye don't have time."

"Please take good care of him. And give him some carrots. He loves carrots."

The line went dead.

Chapter 19

It was the longest day of Patrick's life. He went through his chores with little awareness of what he was doing. He often stopped and looked around, wondering how he had arrived at a certain spot and what he was doing there. By the evening, when he should have been heading home, he went, instead, to the farmhouse.

The office had been turned into Garda headquarters. Several officers were in the room. Some were on the phone, others were pushing papers or just milling around. The local news had picked up on the story, and several horsemen, breeders mostly, were in the room talking with Bran and one another.

Neither Darren Murphy, nor anyone in his family, was seen about.

Patrick quietly slipped into the room, going unnoticed in all the hubbub. He stepped over to the corner nearest the door and listened.

"Any clues as to who committed this grievous act?" said a woman looking up at Bran while sitting on the leather couch in the center of the room.

"The Garda be guessin' the IRA be responsible," said Bran. "But neither the IRA nor anyone else has taken responsibility fer it."

"Seems odd," said the woman. "They have always stepped forward whenever there was a kidnapping. They almost brag about it."

"Perhaps with the love the Irish have fer their hearses, and Fionn in particular," said Bran, scratching the stubble on his chin, "they felt it would be a bad public relations move."

"I suppose that is right," she said, taking a sip of her drink. "Tell me," she added, "what is the Garda doing to find Fionn?"

"Aside from setting up checkpoints on main roads, and searching local farms, they be hopin' somethin' comes of the negotiations with the kidnappers."

Patrick turned his attention to a conversation going on among a group of men, many of whom he recognized as influential breeders.

"The Irish Thoroughbred Breeders Association be one hundred percent against the payment of a ransom. If the kidnappers think they can get money out of us, every hearse in Ireland will be in danger," one man said, tapping his cigar in the ashtray on the table. Patrick recognized the man as William Carroll, the man who had wanted to purchase Fionn and Far and Away Farm a few years previous.

"My sentiments, exactly," said another man standing across from him.

Bran approached the group. "I understand what ye be sayin', but I be still hopin' I can raise the money somehow. Does this mean I won't get any money from the Association?"

"Sure yer owner has all da money in the werld," said Carroll. "He not be willin' ta part wit any of it?"

"The last I heard from him was that he had no intention of coughing up any ransom atol,"

Gallagher said, his voice reflecting the stress he was feeling. He pulled a handkerchief from his pocket and wiped his brow.

"Well now dat does surprise me considerin' he was willin' to pay a fair bit for Far and Away Farm and all da hearses here, including Fionn," said Carroll before he returned to sucking on his cigar. "Sure if he didn't care about the hearse, why didn't he just giv'm ta me when I offered?"

Gallagher didn't have an answer. He merely dropped his chin and walked away.

Patrick felt his chest tighten and he thought, *There must be some way to save Fionn. But if no one will come up with the money, then how?*

The next morning the second call came in. Sir Gallagher again took the call. The Garda gathered around him to listen.

"Do ye have the money?" said the voice over the phone, sounding muffled as it had the day before.

"The owner wants proof that the hearse be alive," Bran said, following the instructions he was given by the Garda. "No money until he knows his investment be safe."

The line went dead.

Later that afternoon, a large envelope was taped to the gate of Far and Away Farm. Patrick noticed it flapping in the breeze as he was gathering a mare from the field. He went to investigate. On the envelope was written in large black letters: "Fionn."

Patrick took it and ran to the farmhouse. Entering, he went directly to Sir Gallagher. "I found this on the gate," he said, handing the envelope to the trainer as he struggled to catch his breath.

Bran tore it open and pulled out a glossy black and white photo of Fionn. The distinctive blaze was visible. The whites around the stallion's eyes glaringly exposed, showing the fear the horse was experiencing. Patrick felt his own eyes well up with tears, and his determination to find Fionn was solidified.

Chapter 20

Patrick tossed and turned in his bed, tormented by the image of Fionn in such a state of fear. His heart ached. Unable to sleep, he was still startled when the phone in the kitchen began ringing. The clock in the living room struck 11 P.M. Patrick ran down the stairs and picked up the receiver.

"Yeah?" he said, his voice uncertain.

"Patrick, it be Ronan."

"Ronan! I be so glad ye called, lad," Patrick said, happy to hear the familiar voice of a friend. "Have ye heard the news about Fionn?"

"Aye. That be why I be callin'."

"It be terrible. Just terrible," Patrick said, fearing he might lose control at any minute and start crying.

"Listen up. I chanced to be at a pub tonight. It was a pub on the west side of Belfast that be frequented by members of the IRA."

Patrick felt his heart start to pound. "Go on, lad."

"All the talk was 'bout Fionn. From what I could determine, the IRA be involved somehow."

"That's what the Garda think, too."

"I have a connection with someone in the IRA. Can you get up here tomorrow? I think we should meet with me contact."

"I be on the first train."

Ronan picked up Patrick at the train station that afternoon. "It be all set," Ronan said as soon as Patrick climbed in the car. "We be meetin' me contact at Bittles Bar in downtown Belfast. The historic structure that houses the bar is known as the Flat Iron Building. It was originally called The Shakespeare due to its location in the theater district since the 1800s. It be in an area not frequented by the IRA, so he thinks no one will recognize him." Ronan took a sharp left turn. "In addition, it be a proper good bar!"

A short time later, Patrick and Ronan walked into the uniquely shaped historic bar. Thick drapes hung from the windows. The ceiling and walls were painted red. The bar at the far wall featured shelf upon shelf of colorful bottles of alcohol. They arrived at 4 P.M., well before the evening crowd. The tables were largely empty.

Sitting at a corner table facing them was a short man. He was dressed in a gray, Aran knit sweater. On his head he wore a traditional scally cap in blue plaid. His face sported a short brown beard. Nothing about the man or his attire would cause anyone to look twice. That was the point.

Watching Patrick and Ronan approach, he lifted his mug of brew in acknowledgment.

Ronan pulled out a chair across from the man and motioned for Patrick to do the same. "Thank ye fer meetin' with us," Ronan said.

The man's eyes darted around the room before he nodded his head. "I don't have much time. But I'll tell ye what I know about the Fionn affair." The man's eyes scanned the room once again before he leaned forward. In a hushed voice, barely above a whisper, he started sharing what he knew.

As Ronan's contact talked, Patrick tipped forward, his forearms on the table. He studied the man's face. His skin above the beard was ruddy. His light blue eyes were small and intense. His expression was stoic, showing no emotion. But what he had to say was heart-stopping.

"The IRA was hired to take the hearse. They need money to finance their part in The Troubles. Anything they can get for a ransom will be theirs to keep. That will be on top of what they were paid to steal the hearse." The man stopped and took a sip from his mug, his eyes continuing to search the room.

"Hired?" blurted Patrick, interrupting Ronan's contact. "Someone *hired* the IRA?"

"Aye. This wasn't something the IRA thought of on their own," the man replied. "Da person who hired the IRA also bribed a man at the farm ta cooperate," he continued.

"What? That be impossible," Patrick said, interrupting again. "No one at Far and Away would be a part of this."

"I just tell ye what I hear."

"Who?"

The man shrugged. "An insider is all I know. I don't have a name."

"And what of the hearse? What of Fionn?" asked Patrick.

"The word I get is that the hearse is to be shipped out of the country."

"Shipped where?" asked Patrick, his hands fidgeting, his muscles tense.

"I don't know that. Go to Waterford. See what ye can learn there."

The man abruptly pushed back his chair and stood. Looking down at Patrick he added, "I tell ye this because I love hearses. It not be right to bring them innocent creatures into this mess."

The man turned, walked past their table, and quickly left the bar.

Left alone at the table, Ronan and Patrick looked at one another. Both faces reflected the shock they were feeling.

Patrick opened his mouth to speak but nothing came out. Pressing his lips together, he shook his head.

Ronan placed a hand on his friend's shoulder. "I know what ye be thinkin'. Ye can't believe anyone at Far and Away would be part of this."

"Impossible."

"Perhaps not. Ye certainly can't eliminate the possibility outright."

Patrick paused and looked quizzically at Ronan. "Why would someone hire the IRA ta steal Fionn?" he asked. "Who would do that?" After pausing again, he muttered, "And he said Fionn is ta be shipped out of the country." He shook his head and rubbed his temples. "I don't understand any o' this."

"That beats the alternative," Ronan said, trying to sound reassuring.

Patrick cocked his head. "What mean ye?"

"At least that means they be keepin' him alive."

Patrick dropped his head in his hands. It had never occurred to him that the kidnappers might kill Fionn. That didn't seem to make sense. He would be of no value to them dead. Until that moment his only concern was that Fionn was being fed properly and given a chance to exercise.

He hated to think of him tied up in a musty old barn on some neglected piece of property.

Yet, killing Fionn *was* a possibility. He shoved back his chair and stood. The few customers in the bar looked their way.

"I need ta get home. I have work ta do," he said to Ronan.

Chapter 21

The train ride home was anything but relaxing. Patrick sat in his seat, rubbing his palms on his thighs as he tried to analyze the information he had just been given. His mind was in a whirl.

The first thought that tormented him was the matter of Fionn's safety. The horse-loving IRA man had seemed to be convinced that Fionn would be kept alive and shipped out of the country. But shipped to where? The only thing the man said was to go to Waterford. The port city on the southeast coast of Ireland had a large harbor that serviced imports and exports from around the world. The port had, in the past, run a profitable business shipping livestock, including horses, to Europe and America. Since The Troubles began, it was rumored that the IRA was using the port to ship arms into the country.

The second major concern for Patrick was who at the farm might have helped the kidnappers if, indeed, anyone had. While he still found it hard to believe, he had to admit to himself that it wasn't beyond possibility. With enough money on the table, most people could be bought. Others had ideological beliefs that put them on one side or the other of The Troubles.

Third, he wondered: *Who would do such a thing? Who wanted this horse so badly they'd cut a deal with the IRA?*

Upon returning home, he slept for a couple of hours before reporting to Far and Away Farm. Finding Sir Gallagher in the barn with the stallions, he approached him.

"Sir Gallagher," he said, feeling the nerves turning his stomach over, "be ye available for a brief conversation?"

Sir Gallagher turned on his heel. "Where have ye been?" His voice was filled with irritation, his face creased with annoyance.

Surprised at such a reception, Patrick stepped back. Sir Gallagher's emotions rarely showed through his patient and kind demeanor. "I be sorry. I be called out of town." Something in the trainer's tone left Patrick with the feeling that he should not disclose where he had been. *Can I trust anyone?* he asked himself.

Bran's face and tone of voice softened. "I be the one who is sorry, lad. I haven't had much sleep. But this be hard on everyone. I shouldn't take it out on ye."

"I understand. Sleep has not been me friend, either."

"Add to that, I have had to take over the responsibilities of managing the farm."

"What of Mr. Murphy?"

"Seems he was so frightened by the whole affair he has taken his family and disappeared," Sir Gallagher said. "I guess it not be me right to complain. I might have done the same had I gone through what he did. But enough about me. What did ya want to speak to me about, lad?"

Quickly changing his mind about what he wanted to disclose, Patrick merely said, "Have ye been able to get the ransom money?"

The light went out of Bran's eyes as he dropped his chin and shook his head. "Not enough, I be afraid. The owner won't pay a thing. One of the racing magazines offered ten thousand pounds and the breeders association agreed to contribute fifty thousand pounds. But that be it. The kidnappers have cut off all communication. I be afraid Fionn be lost to us forever."

Patrick sat down on a tack trunk and clutched his hands. He glanced over at Fionn's empty stall and let the tears flow freely.

Sir Gallagher stepped up to him and put an arm over his shoulder. "Why don't ye take a few days off? Go get some rest."

Patrick sniffed. "Yeah. I need to. But so do ye."

"I need to be here in case the kidnappers call . . . though the Garda don't think they will. The officer in charge of the investigation has quit doing press conferences. They've quit manning the roadblocks." Bran sighed. "Can't blame 'em really. To them he's just a hearse."

"Aren't the people putting pressure on them to find Fionn?"

"Yeah. Lots of pressure. But pressure won't bring Fionn home."

Chapter 22

Mrs. McCallin was surprised to see Patrick home so early in the day. "Be ye sick?" she asked, as any mother would.

"Sir Gallagher sent me home ta get some rest, though he be in need of rest more than I."

"Be there news 'bout Fionn?" she asked, delicately.

Patrick dropped his chin and shook his head. "The Garda has pretty much given up, and the kidnappers have not called back."

Mrs. McCallin stepped forward and embraced her son. Though not a horsewoman herself, she understood the love that the men in her family had for the magnificent beasts. "I wish there be something I could do to help ye," she whispered.

Patrick pulled back and looked in his mother's blue eyes. "There is."

She smiled. "Wonderful. What be that?"

"Ye can let me take the car to Waterford ta follow up on a lead I received when I met with Ronan and his acquaintance."

His mother's eyes opened wide. "Waterford? I hear there be much IRA activity in that area. Do ye think it be safe?"

"I'll watch me step. Ye needn't fear fer me," Patrick said, giving his mother's hand a tight squeeze.

Her knotted brows showed she wasn't convinced. But she handed over the car keys anyway.

A short time later, Patrick threw a satchel in the boot and, telling his mother he would be gone for a day or two, drove off their property and down the road. He headed south on the island, sometimes on tiny country roads, sometimes on the main road, toward the southeast coast where Waterford was located. His mind was a jumble of thoughts. He wasn't quite sure why he was going to Waterford, or what he would find there. Only that the IRA contact told him to go.

Weak sunlight filtered through the constant drizzle as he drove. He passed through villages whose tiny houses lining the streets had been built decades before. Village after village petered out and opened into the countryside covered with a carpet of bright green grasses and ancient oak and beech trees. His attention was drawn to every horse and barn he passed. *Could Fionn be there? Did the Garda search that barn?* In several places, the hedgerows had grown so wild the road became too narrow for cars to pass one another and hid the farms from view. It seemed to Patrick that hiding a horse could be an easy thing to do.

He arrived at the port town of Waterford, Ireland's oldest city, just before dinnertime and just as he was about to run out of petrol. He felt his muscles tighten and his nerves set on edge the minute he drove into town. Nosing around an IRA stronghold wasn't exactly the safest thing to do. He suddenly wished he had brought Ronan along. He distracted himself by looking for a petrol station.

With the tank filled up, he drove down Bradley's New Street and parked just down the road from a local pub called *The Munster Bar*. It had the reputation for being one of the oldest, if not *the* oldest, pub in Waterford, having served as a tavern since 1853. His stomach had been growling for over an hour, and the thought of some fresh fish and chips was just what he needed.

He entered the pub and breathed in deeply the smell of fried fish wafting from the kitchen. The dark paneled walls and woodwork, along with the numerous, glowing candelabras, filled the tavern with a warm and welcoming feel. He found a small round table near the bar and sat down. A young woman took his order and returned a short time later with a plate full of freshly fried fish and chips.

She smiled at Patrick as she set the plate in front of him. "Ye be visitin'?"

"Yeah."

"What ye here ta see?"

"I be curious about the shipping industry."

"Ah-h-h. That be a big part of the city . . . that and the crystal factory," she said, brushing a golden lock out of her eyes and pinning it behind one ear.

"And ye? Been here long?" he asked before shoving a large slice of fried potato into his mouth.

"Born and raised. Me family, the Fitzgeralds, have owned the pub fer two generations."

Patrick thought he would take a chance. "Have ye noticed any strangers or unusual activity in town?"

"Be ye jokin'? That be a common occurrence me whole life."

"Yer whole life?" Patrick said, curious about her meaning.

"Ye know. Ever since The Troubles began."

Patrick nodded with understanding. "Can ye tell me if there be anything that seemed particularly odd last week?"

The young girl looked from side to side, inspecting the room, before she answered. "Well, it seems there be more whispered conversations 'round the tables the past few days. I don't know what it all means. Just somethin' me noticed."

"Did ye catch anything being said?"

Her hand went to her chest aghast. "What? Me? I would never presume ta eavesdrop on me customers."

After a filling dinner, Patrick found his way to Dooley's, a hotel in the center of town. The hotel with its red brick façade and a painting of a ship on the upper floor was easy to find. The old and popular establishment boasted soft beds and a full Irish breakfast, both of which he soon found to be true.

The rooks in the old chestnut tree behind the hotel put up a ruckus that awakened Patrick from a dreamless sleep. Surprised that he had slept so long, he hurried and dressed. He dashed down the stairs to grab a bite of breakfast before setting off to explore the old town and seaport. He quickly discovered that there would be no dashing to be had. He was seated at a table near the window, not far from a comforting fireplace, and promptly brought a plate piled high with bacon strips, called "rashers," fried eggs, baked tomatoes, shredded and grilled potatoes, and a loaf of freshly baked soda bread. As he ate his hearty meal, he listened to the chatter of the patrons around him. From what they were saying, it appeared most were businessmen or salesmen. Not a word was said about The Troubles and the IRA or Fionn.

Stepping out the door after the delicious breakfast, he was met with a strong wind blowing the raindrops sideways. He smiled as he thought of his mother's oft repeat of the old Irish saying: "There be only three types of weather in Ireland: It's raining, it has just rained, or it is soon to rain."

Patrick zipped up his jacket and hurried to his car. He drove down to the waterfront, which was abuzz with activity. Fishermen and their boats were zipping around large freight vessels docked in the harbor. Carts and trucks rolled along the front street, filled with crates going to and from the ships.

He found a parking spot on a narrow, cobblestone side road, and headed toward the docks, passing several whitewashed buildings tucked next to one another and separated from the street by a narrow sidewalk.

A large building just off the main road bore a sign that read: "Waterford Harbour

Commissioners." Patrick rubbed his hands together to warm them and entered the building.

A pleasant older woman smiled at him by way of greeting. "May I help ye?"

"Yes. I would like ta speak ta the Commissioner," Patrick said, brushing the raindrops off his shoulders.

Pushing her glasses up the bridge of her nose, she looked down at her appointment book. "Do ye have an appointment?"

"No."

"In that case, I'll write ye in at 10 o'clock," she said, grabbing a pen. "What be yer name?"

"Patrick McCallin."

The woman looked up. "The famous Jockey?"

"Jockey, yeah. 'Famous' be questionable."

"Well, around here ye certainly be famous. Wait 'till I tell me family I met ye. They'll be green with envy."

Patrick blushed and dropped his eyes to his fidgeting hands.

"May I know the nature of yer visit?" she said, reverting to her position as receptionist.

"I have some questions fer him about shipping livestock."

She nodded as she scribbled in her appointment book. Dotting the period with a flair, she said, "There! All set. The Commissioner will see ye at 10. Don't be late. He be a very busy man."

"Thank you. I'll be back."

Having an hour to kill, Patrick decided to walk along the docks. He marveled at the huge ships being unloaded. Giant cranes lifted crates from the ships and swung them over to the docks before men unhooked them and the process repeated itself. It was fascinating to watch such precision and efficiency.

He tried to imagine what it would be like to put Fionn on one of those ships, and he felt his heart flutter with fear.

At exactly 10 a.m., Patrick was led into the office of Michael O'Reilly, the Harbor Commissioner for Waterford. He was a short, plump man dressed in a smart-looking navy-blue uniform. He was seated behind his cluttered desk, but he stood when Patrick entered the room. Smiling, he extended his hand. "Pleased ta meet ye, Mr. McCallin."

"Thank ye," Patrick said, shaking the proffered hand.

"Please sit. Tea?"

Patrick shook his head. "No, thank ye."

"Well, then, let's get down to business, shall we? What would ye like ta discuss?"

Patrick cleared his throat. He had rehearsed what he was going to say for the last hour. "Sir, I have heard rumors that Fionn, the famous racehorse who has disappeared, might have been shipped out of the country through Waterford."

Patrick assumed O'Reilly had heard of the kidnapping. By now, everyone in Ireland, and probably beyond, knew of the crime.

O'Reilly, who had just taken a sip of his tea, spit it out over the papers on his desk. "Ach! Ye heard what?"

"I heard that Fionn was shipped out of the country from yer port," Patrick said, leaning forward on the edge of his chair.

"And from whom did ye hear this?" O'Reilly asked, his eyes locked on Patrick's eyes while leaning forward and dabbing up the tea with his handkerchief.

"From a member of the IRA."

O'Reilly's face registered surprise as he sat back in his chair. "Be that so?"

"It be well known that the IRA is smuggling arms into Ireland from Waterford."

The Commissioner pursed his lips and wrinkled his brow. He nodded slowly. "We be doing our best ta stop it, but we can't open every crate that comes in here."

"I understand. But tell me. Be it possible that Fionn could have been shipped out of here?"

O'Reilly removed his glasses and set them carefully on his desk. His jaw twitched as he gazed around his utilitarian office, appearing to be considering his response. The thought crossed Patrick's mind that he might know more than he was willing to share.

Finally, O'Reilly spoke. "We handled quite a few hearses here at Waterford up until a few years ago. At that time, it would have been quite easy ta add a horse ta a shipment of livestock without anyone payin' it any mind. But today it would be quite difficult because of the constant monitoring and examination of all livestock."

"Ye said 'difficult.' Does that mean it wouldn't be impossible?" asked Patrick, feeling his heart beating faster.

"I should have said it would be *very* difficult, but not impossible. However, it would be more likely that if, and that be a big *IF*, the hearse were ta be smuggled out of the country by ship, it would more likely be through one of the numerous small coves. They be so isolated, it be impossible fer me and me staff ta monitor movement in and out of all of them."

Chapter 23

Before Patrick left, the Commissioner suggested he might want to explore an area called Dunmore East.

Patrick thanked O'Reilly for his help and returned to his car. Thinking about the Commissioner's comments, he was convinced that Fionn could very well have been shipped out of the country, perhaps through one of the fishing villages along the coast. Why the Commissioner had suggested Dunmore East, he didn't know. But he was determined to find out.

He drove along the coastline to Dunmore East. Situated to the west of Waterford along the southeast coast of Ireland, the area around the village had once been settled by the Vikings and Normans. The port was nothing like that in Waterford. No large ocean-going vessels would be able to dock there. Only smaller fishing vessels were seen tied to the old, and often dilapidated, piers.

The lovely cove around which the village was situated boasted a sandy beach, currently empty of visitors, and whitewashed homes built right up to the sea wall. Lush green, rolling fields extended beyond the homes to the north as far as the eye could see. Rows of deciduous trees, currently bare of leaves, formed natural windbreaks between the fields. Just beyond was the harbor, its oceanside entrance marked by an ancient lighthouse. Patrick headed to the carpark by the harbor.

A stiff wind was blowing off the water, carrying the smell of salt and fish as Patrick climbed out of the car. Happily, the rain had stopped for the time being. He paused and looked from side to side, still not sure where to go or with whom to speak.

Being a Wednesday, the pier was crowded with fishermen preparing to go out, intending to return on Thursday with a full catch to send to market for Friday sales. Ireland, being a Catholic country, still had many people who observed what was once, but no longer, a church requirement. It had now become a cultural tradition to eat fish on Friday, and Friday Fish Fries were popular social gatherings.

Patrick walked to the docks. There he found numerous fishermen baiting their lobster traps and preparing fish nets. Hard labor meant there was always someone willing to take a break and visit with an "inlander." Wishing he had read more Sherlock Holmes novels as a boy so he would know how to question people, he shrugged his shoulders and approached the nearest person.

The man was working on untangling a large fishing net. His brow was beaded with sweat. As Patrick approached, the man stood and pressed his hands to his aching back. He stretched and let out a soft groan. Looking at Patrick, he smiled. "Greetings, mate."

Patrick struck up a conversation about fishing, asking questions and getting more detail in the responses than he could ever want. Eventually, he gathered up the nerve to ask about Fionn. "Me friends tell me they heard the famous racehorse, Fionn, was taken out o' here."

The man's face blanched white. "I can't help ye there, lad." Then he did something that shocked Patrick. He turned and shouted out to the line of fishermen working around him. "This lad's lookin' fer Fionn."

This caught everyone's attention. Nets and traps were abandoned, and a large group of men gathered around the visitor. Patrick's face turned ashen, and the hair on the back of his neck and arms lifted. He pressed his lips tightly together to keep them from trembling.

"Go on," said the first man. "Tell 'em what ye told me."

Patrick took a shuddering breath before speaking. "I have friends who told me they heard Fionn be taken out o' the country from Dunmore East."

A burst of laughter erupted from the men.

Patrick looked from face to face, confused as to what the laughter meant.

One burly man, smelling strongly of fish, stepped forward, his face a sneer. Patrick felt himself shrink in fear. "Well, lad, if that happened, ye'll nye hear it from the likes o' us. Ye best be movin' on. We don't take kindly to strangers nosin' 'round our business."

Patrick blinked and gave the man a quick nod. The crowd of men parted, and Patrick made a hasty retreat to his car. He climbed into the driver's seat and let out a long breath of air he hadn't realized he was holding. Placing his hands and forehead on the steering wheel, he tried to calm his pounding heart.

A rap on the window caused him to jump. He looked over to see a young lass smiling at him. Cracking the window slightly, he raised his eyebrows in acknowledgment.

"Meet me at Powers Bar on Dock Road at 11, after the fishin' boats have left." She turned and hurried up the street.

Chapter 24

A few minutes before 11, Patrick walked in the front door of the popular eating and drinking establishment called *Powers Bar*, located on the main road, halfway between the pier and the beach. The interior reminded him of the Munster Bar he had visited the night before, with the exception of the row of windows affording a view of the water. The rich dark wood paneling and the dim lighting made for a cozy atmosphere. The smell of fish signaled the restaurant's specialty.

Vaguely remembering what the young woman looked like, he searched the faces of the customers. An attractive, young woman lifted her hand and caught his attention. Walking over to the table, Patrick said, "Be ye the one who summoned me?"

"That be me," she said, her eyes twinkling, her smile showing off straight, white teeth. "Ye met me friend wit works at The Munster Bar. She said to be on the lookout for ye, Mr. Patrick McCallin, the famous jockey."

"Excuse me, but I seem to be at the disadvantage. Somehow, ye know me name, but I don't know yers."

"I be Kylie Walsh. Me friend knew who you be – nearly everyone in all of Ireland knows who ye be. Sit down and buy me lunch and I will tell ye what I know."

Patrick followed Kylie's lead and ordered a bowl of fish chowder. As they ate, Kylie talked in a whisper, frequently glancing around the room.

"Ye be looking for yer hearse," she stated.

Patrick nodded.

"I respect that. I be a hearse-lover, and not a bad rider, if I do say so meself."

She took several spoonfuls of the soup. Patrick watched her, impatience rising inside. "Ye said ye had something to tell me?" he said, prodding.

"Yeah," she said, setting down her spoon and wiping her mouth with her napkin. "I know there be a large shipment of arms that came into port two nights after Fionn went missing."

"For the IRA?"

She looked down at her soup, took another spoonful of chowder, and nodded.

"But what does that have to do with Fionn."

She glanced around the room again before bending forward and whispering, "Payment."

"Payment for Fionn?" Patrick whispered back.

She nodded.

"Are ye sayin' Fionn was stolen by the IRA in exchange fer arms? Are ye sure 'bout this?"

"Let's just say I put two and two together. I be around long enough to know how this works."

"But who hired them to take the hearse?"

Kylie shrugged.

"Do ye know where Fionn be now?"

She shook her head. "I only know what I hear. In the early hours of the very night after Fionn was stolen, an all-black hearse was put aboard an old drifter type boat that has a bigger hatch than the boats the fishermen use now."

"Fionn isn't black."

Kylie smirked. "Ever heard o' hair dye?"

Patrick's stomach churned and he pushed the bowl of chowder away, suddenly losing his appetite. *All this time the Garda had been looking for a bay horse with a blaze down his face and four white socks. All the kidnappers had to do was alter his appearance and they could get past any checkpoint.*

"*Buíochas.* Thank ye fer sharin' this information with me," Patrick said as he pulled out his wallet and paid for the lunch.

"I hope ye find yer hearse, Patrick McCallin."

Patrick shook his head. "It be a big world, and ye just made me realize how big."

"Yeah," Kylie said, her eyelids dropping.

As Patrick turned to leave the pub, Kylie called out, "Éire go Deo," the Irish motto meaning "Forever Ireland."

Patrick didn't look back as he raised his arm and waved his hand, then pushed his way through the incoming customers and out the door.

Chapter 25

While Patrick drove north to Kildare, his spirit was deflated. Hopelessness was his foremost emotion. Convinced, now, that Fionn had been shipped out of Ireland and that the IRA had something to do with it, he was left with the realization that his precious horse could be just about anywhere. He paid little attention to the countryside whizzing past as his mind raced with the possibilities.

Was the IRA acting on its own? Or was it hired, as Kylie asserted, to kidnap Fionn? The IRA had used kidnapping as a tool to raise funds in the past, but they had always claimed responsibility for the action. That had not happened with Fionn.

Perhaps they were keeping quiet because they knew it would not be received well by the Irish people who loved Fionn and saw him as a national hero.

Or was an enemy of Fionn's absent owner responsible? Perhaps a jealous competitor wanted to punish Fionn's owner or wanted to use Fionn to improve their own stock. Thoroughbred breeders from Ireland to Europe, from the Middle East to America, had tried to purchase Fionn. Could one of those men or women have been responsible for this rash act?

Or might the owner have arranged the kidnapping himself to collect insurance money? That would explain why he refused to pay the ransom. Yet, did that make sense? The horse was providing him with a handsome profit as a stud. There was a bevy of outstanding mares lined up for the upcoming breeding season. Breeders were paying up to £80,000 to breed their mares to the famous Fionn.

The only bright spot in all he had learned during his trip to Waterford was that Fionn was most probably alive.

As Patrick mulled over the possibilities of what had befallen Fionn in Ireland, Maddie was facing her own worries in France. The news of Fionn's kidnapping had spread around the world, and not just in the racing circles. It seemed everyone had a heart for the horse and devoured any news the media could conjure up. Maddie, with her connection to Patrick and RACE was one of those. So, when an odd thing happened at her stable, her suspicions were on high alert.

After graduating from RACE with a stable management certification, she returned to her home in Lille, in the north of France. A local stable in Hem, a lovely and quaint village just a twenty-five-minute drive from her home, was looking for a manager for its growing business. She happily took the job.

The stable, named Westwind Farm, offered a full range of services, from riding instruction to boarding and training. The success of the horses and riders at the local shows was bringing attention to the stable, and the business was growing. New horses arrived weekly for boarding and training, and new students and owners came for instruction. Maddie's responsibilities included not only the care of the horses and grounds but also a full load of students.

Thus, it was not anything unusual when Maddie arrived at work several days earlier to find a new horse in one of the stalls.

He was a magnificent, all-black stallion.

Maddie marveled at the beauty of the new horse. His lean lines and long, muscular body signaled that he was a Thoroughbred. She immediately recognized the quality of his breeding.

Her first task was to move him to a separate barn where he could be away from the mares and geldings. Before she left the main barn to prepare a stall in the stallion barn, she decided to get the horse a clean bucket of water. Walking to the water spigot she was surprised to hear what seemed to be a familiar voice coming from the office. She stopped outside the closed door and listened. She bit her lip and held her breath. She *did* know that voice.

"Ye received the payment then?"

"*Oui*. His board is paid in full."

"I suspect he be here for only 'bout a month – just until the owner has settled into his new farm."

"Of course, monsieur. Rest assured that he will have only the best of care."

It wasn't the sound of the barn owner, speaking English with a French accent, that caught Maddie's attention. It was the other voice, with its unmistakable Irish lilt. She knew that voice from her time at RACE when she and Patrick visited Far and Away Farm. It was Darren Murphy. She was sure of it.

Hearing the men approaching the door while saying their goodbyes, she hurried down the aisleway, stopping at the faucet to fill the bucket. Keeping her back to the approaching man and her head down, she let him pass, glancing up only long enough to confirm that her suspicions were correct.

Darren Murphy? What could he be doing here? Is he no longer employed at Far and Away? And the new horse? He must have brought him here. But who is the horse's owner?

It was certainly not unusual for managers and trainers to move from one stable to another, just as coaches move from one football team to another in the U.S. So, Maddie put her concerns aside and went about her responsibilities: ordering feed, organizing turnout, and teaching her students the correct position over jumps. But then something happened that changed all that.

The black stallion had been at the stable for two or three days when Maddie went to retrieve him from turnout in a lower pasture far from the other horses. The rain had been falling unceasingly for the entire day, but the horse had enjoyed his time out of his stall, frolicking across the wet fields and rolling in the sticky mud.

"Oh, my goodness, boy, you have certainly made a mess of yourself," she said while placing the headstall over his head and clipping on the lead. "Looks like you are due for a good hosing off and rubdown."

Maddie led the stallion back to the small barn where he was housed and clipped him to the cross-ties in the wash stall. She hosed him down with warm water, grabbed some dry towels, and began to rub him down. It was then that it happened. As she lifted the towel from his firm body, she noticed that the fabric was black. Not black from the mud. This looked different. She grabbed a clean towel and started rubbing again. The new towel was covered in black as well. She went to his head and started rubbing his face. As she rubbed, the hair on his face began to show streaks of white. Shocked, she stepped back and looked more closely at the horse.

It couldn't be, could it?

She grabbed another towel and rubbed his face until a wide white blaze was clearly exposed from his eyes to his nostrils — a blaze that was familiar to all horse racing enthusiasts.

With more work, four white socks appeared above the sturdy hooves.

Chapter 26

As soon as Patrick returned home, he was greeted by his mother. "Oh, me boy. I be so worried about ye. Did ye find out anything that be of help?"

Patrick nodded; his thoughts were still melancholy.

"Well," said his mother, her son's gloomy outlook not lost on her. "I have news for ye that will brighten yer spirits."

Patrick looked up into her laughing eyes.

"Yer friend from France, Maddie, called. She be very anxious ta talk ta ye."

Patrick debated about calling Maddie. He wasn't sure he had the energy to be friendly. But, with his mother's prodding, he picked up the receiver and dialed Maddie's number.

Maddie answered the phone and without preamble got right to the point. "Patrick, I need you to come to Lille. I've found Fionn."

The ferry to Cherbourg, in Normandy, left the next afternoon from Rosslare. Patrick's grandfather drove him to the port situated on the eastern coast of Ireland. Patrick boarded the ferry and waved "Goodbye." He watched Grandfather return to the carpark before going to find his cabin. The trip by ferry would take eighteen hours. Though much slower than a plane, it was much less expensive. Patrick had no choice but to take the slower route.

As they set off along the St. Georges Channel that separates the Irish Sea from the Celtic Sea, the clouds blew in and the sky darkened. When the captain steered the ferry south into the Celtic Sea, the blustering winds unsettled the waters, and the ferry began to rock. Patrick went on deck to try to calm his stomach, and remained there as they rounded the tip of Wales and headed toward England. The wind increased, stirring up the waves with it. A salty spray washed over Patrick as he stood by the railing.

"The horses of *Manannán mac Lir*," Patrick mumbled, as he watched the white-crested waves of the sea. The froth and foam at the top of wild waves reminded the early Irish settlers of galloping horses. Thus, they were thought to be the steeds belonging to the Irish sea deity, *Manannán mac Lir*, the guardian between worlds.

Wrapping his scarf tightly around his neck, the young man used the ends of his scarf to wipe the sea spray from his face. The ferry beat on against the current as the darkness of the sky and the black water melded into one.

Tired from the day of travel and his churning thoughts that denied him any peace, Patrick decided there was nothing to do but return to his cabin and try to get some sleep.

Back in his cabin, he did his best to remain on his feet as he changed into night clothes. A crashing wave tipped the boat, and Patrick found himself sprawled across his bed. With a sigh of frustration, he shoved his feet in the pant legs and crawled under the thin, wool blanket. Gripping the sides of the bunk, he stared at the ceiling, trying to calm his stomach. He held himself in the bed for what seemed several hours.

As he lay on his cot, the intensity of his emotions, waxing and waning like the moon itself, kept him from sleeping. The hopelessness he felt while returning from Waterford that had so weighed him down was replaced with elation at the news that Maddie had found Fionn. But the elation was quickly transformed to fear and doubt. *How would he and Maddie be able to swoop in and rescue the world's most famous horse without getting caught? The people who stole him played for keeps, and their partnership with the IRA showed just how desperate and determined they were.*

Sometime during the darkest part of the night, the captain steered the ferry around the tip of England and into the English Channel that separates Great Britain from France. About that time, sleep found Patrick where he lay clutching the sides of his bunk.

The morning dawned bright and clear, though the air was crisp. The seagulls swarmed the dock in Cherbourg looking for handouts as Patrick disembarked. Following Maddie's directions, he found his way to the train station and purchased a ticket to Lille. Within the hour, Patrick was seated on the train as it left the station.

The five-hour ride to Lille proved to be restful as the rhythmic clicking of the wheels on the track and the gentle sway of the cars rocked him to sleep. He missed the charming countryside and small towns as the train traveled toward Lille, situated in the northeast corner of France, near the border between France and Belgium. Charming Lille had been famous for its lace-making for centuries. But lace was not what Patrick would be looking for, nor what he was dreaming of.

The conductor shook his shoulder, and Patrick groaned and stirred.

"We have arrived at Lille," the uniformed man said in his French accent.

Patrick's eyes shot open. "Ach!" he said jumping up. "Thank ye."

"*De rien, monsieur*. I didn't want you to miss your stop."

Patrick grabbed his bag and walked up the aisle to the end of the car. He stepped out of the train and onto the platform. Passengers were moving about in all directions, some greeting one another, others hurrying on their way. Patrick looked both ways, searching for Maddie's familiar face.

At last, he saw her stepping through the depot door. Spotting her before she noticed him, Patrick hurried down the platform. "Maddie," he called.

Maddie turned toward the sound of Patrick's voice. Her pursed lips stretched into the wide smile Patrick loved. She ran toward him, arms outstretched. She wrapped her arms around Patrick, pinching his arms to his side.

Patrick laughed. "Ye be squishin' me."

Releasing her hold, she stepped back and looked into his eyes. The smile disappeared from her face and tears welled in her eyes and spilled down her cheeks. "I am so relieved that you came. I couldn't handle this by myself. I don't even know what to do."

"Let's get ta the car and we'll talk about it there," Patrick said.

Chapter 27

They walked through the carpark without saying a word, Maddie several steps ahead. She stopped at the back of her little, tan Renault and opened the trunk. "You can throw your bag in here," she said.

Climbing into the cramped front seat, Maddie started the car. As soon as Patrick climbed in the passenger seat and buckled in, she backed up and spun out of the lot. Patrick was glad for his short stature as he struggled to get comfortable in the little car.

"Alright, Maddie. Tell me what happened," Patrick said.

Her face was etched with concern as she began telling Patrick all that had happened since the mysterious black stallion arrived at Westwind Farm. Patrick stared at her in disbelief as she related the story.

"Darren Murphy be involved?" he said, finding it hard to accept.

Maddie pursed her lips and nodded.

"But who be he workin' fer?"

"I don't know. And I haven't seen him at the barn since that first day when the horse was brought in."

"Does anyone know ye have discovered Fionn's true identity?"

"No one. I have told no one. I'm too frightened. You were the only person I dared to call."

Patrick looked out the side window, not paying any attention to the charming and historic town of Lille as they drove through it.

The heavy late-day traffic on the Louis XIV Boulevard came to a stop. "Oh, dear. We could be stuck in traffic for hours at this rate. I'm getting off the boulevard," Maddie said. Gripping the steering wheel, she turned off onto a narrow side street lined with charming, old four- and five-story buildings with street-level shops and restaurants, and apartments in the floors above.

A short distance ahead, the road circled a giant, grandiose triumphal arch that towered over a small opening with a drawbridge. The beautiful structure caught Patrick's attention and pulled him out of his contemplation long enough to ask, "What be that?"

"That is the *Porte de Paris*, which means Paris Gate. It was built in the late 1600s after King Louis XIV seized Lille from the Spanish control of the then-Flemish city. It was once a part of a great wall the French built to defend the city."

As they drove around the circle, Patrick marveled at the ornate Baroque-style architecture. Even the charming castles in Ireland couldn't compete with this in beauty. "Amazing," he whispered.

They continued to wend their way east on the narrow streets of old Lille before breaking free of the traffic and getting on N356, the main highway that would take them to Hem.

The drive to Hem took only twenty minutes once they were out of the city. The time was used to formulate a plan.

"I feel we need to disguise Fionn again," Maddie said. "I don't want Mr. Murphy to learn that I discovered his identity."

"That be true," Patrick said. "How do we do that?"

Maddie motioned with her head toward the back seat where there was a shopping bag. "I bought some more hair dye."

"And once he be disguised, then what?" Patrick asked.

"I have a friend that owns a stable in Wattrelos. I would like to take Fionn there after we disguise him again. We can notify the authorities once we have him safely away from the people who stole him."

"Ye don't want ta go ta the police now?"

Maddie looked over at Patrick with a sly smile on her face. "I want to find out who's behind this. If we tell the police now, Darren Murphy and the mysterious man behind all of this will disappear in the sunset and never be caught. They might even try to dispose of Fionn to cover up what they have done. We'll never know why or how they kidnapped Fionn other than we know they had Darren Murphy's help."

"And the IRA."

Maddie opened her eyes wide in surprise. "The IRA? What are you talking about?"

"I went to Waterford at the recommendation of an acquaintance of Ronan. There I talked ta several people. Some were forthcoming about their suspicions that the IRA received payment in arms fer kidnappin' Fionn. Others refused ta give me information and clearly threatened me."

Maddie shook her head in disgust. "Kidnapping businessmen is one thing. Kidnapping an innocent horse is something else entirely!"

"Me sentiments, exactly," Patrick said. He looked over at her and chuckled. "I didn't know ye be such a detective at heart!"

Chapter 28

As Maddie and Patrick drove through Lille, they proceeded along the narrow streets of the oldest part of the town. Unbeknownst to them they passed directly by a bistro in which Darren Murphy sat waiting for a man he had yet to meet.

Murphy had a picture of the person but no name. That did not surprise or bother him. Ever since this whole affair started, names, or at least given names, were not used.

He had been contacted by members of the IRA in early January. They offered him a very large sum of money to help with their latest fundraising venture. That was the way they had put it — a fundraising venture. As he listened to their plan and the role he was to play, he realized this would be a life-changing event for both him and his family. It would mean betraying his current boss and moving his family to another country. But it also meant that he would become a far wealthier man than serving as the head groom at a stable would ever afford him.

The negotiations were brief. He had little to bargain with. It quickly became apparent that either he cooperated, or his family would be in danger. The fact that they were willing to pay him, as well as relocate his family, was considered a bonus in his mind.

His only task was to make sure there were no security features added to the property, which included no locks on the gates, and to help the men load Fionn once they arrived. Only after the theft of Fionn were additional tasks added to the list.

Murphy had secured a promise that neither Fionn nor his family would be harmed. Thus, when the masked and armed men appeared at his home, he was taken aback. He wasn't sure what he expected, but he certainly didn't expect that.

Fear for his family led him to regret that he had trusted a band of mercenaries in the first place.

The man he was supposed to meet was late. Murphy ordered a drink and a sandwich to tide him over, having had nothing to eat since he left his family at midday in their temporary home located a couple of hours away. As he waited, he mulled over the days since the kidnapping.

The day after the kidnapping, as Sir Gallagher was fielding the phone call with the ransom demand, he had taken his own call. Apparently, none of the kidnappers knew how to handle a horse, especially not a high-spirited animal such as Fionn. If Murphy was to receive his payment, he would have to continue to help them.

After hustling his family out of Ireland and moving them to France, he had been obligated to find suitable stabling for the horse while the mysterious owner, the man who hired both him and the IRA, purchased a permanent farm on which the horse would live out his life. He didn't learn the name of that man until he landed in France and took possession of Fionn from the fishermen who had been paid handsomely to ferry Fionn from Dunmore East in Ireland to an equally small port on the northern coast of France.

Now that he knew the identity of the man behind it all, he understood. He knew how competitive the racehorse breeding business had become. He also knew that money talked. If someone had enough money, they usually got what they wanted. If that person didn't get what they wanted, they never forgot and rarely forgave. Now he was in the middle of it all.

He finished his sandwich and checked his watch again, irritation rising and written on his face as his jaw clenched. Just as he motioned for his check, a large, muscular man in a black wool overcoat entered the pub and walked directly toward him. Murphy felt his muscles tighten and he clutched the water glass he held in his hand until his knuckles were white.

"Murphy?" the man said after stopping in front of his table.

Murphy nodded once in acknowledgment.

"I be sent to ensure the delivery of the goods goes smooth," said the man, not waiting for an invitation before he sat in the chair across from Murphy.

Murphy watched the large man as he ordered a pint of Guinness. He swigged down the "black stuff," as it is called in Ireland, and lowered the empty mug down to the table. Only then did he look Murphy in the eye.

"Let's be goin' about our business, shall we?" the man said to Murphy.

"What do ye know about hearses?" Murphy asked in a whisper as he glanced around the room to see if anyone was paying attention to them.

"Nothing. But I have other skills that might be needed."

Murphy looked over the man with his barrel chest and arms the size of footballs. He felt his heart race, but he forced himself to nod slowly.

"Did ye secure the hearse box?" Murphy whispered.

"Yes. I be sure ye will find it satisfactory."

Chapter 29

It was just past feeding time when Maddie and Patrick pulled into the drive leading to Westwind Farm. The sun was sinking in the west and a sliver of a moon was just making its appearance as they climbed out of the Renault. The scent of horses floated on the gentle breeze as they hurried toward the small white barn where Fionn was stabled. From a distant treetop, an owl's hoot penetrated the quiet of the approaching night.

Patrick felt his heart pounding in anticipation of seeing Fionn again. He hurried ahead of Maddie, opened the barn door, and walked quickly down the aisle, searching each stall.

At last, he found him. "Fionn," he whispered, a wave of both relief and elation washing over him.

Hearing him, Fionn raised his head from his hay manger, his ears pricked forward, and his eyes sparkled in recognition.

Patrick threw open the stall door and, with a forced calmness, approached the horse. Fionn rubbed his muzzle against his jockey's chest and Patrick responded by throwing his arms around the stallion's neck.

"Ye be safe, Fionn! Me prayers have been answered this night."

The reunion was short and sweet as Maddie entered the stall with a bucket of hair dye. "Let's get him black again," she said, handing Patrick a sponge.

It took a lot of work as the two friends spread black liquid over Fionn, hiding his white blaze and white socks and turning his brown coat to black. But an hour or so later, the deed was done, and Patrick and Maddie left his stall to do their best to remove the dye from their hands. They returned a short time later to remove the wet, blackened straw and replace it with fresh bedding.

"Let's get to bed," Maddie said, wiping the perspiration from her forehead. "We need to get an early start in the morning."

Well before sunup, Maddie drove her brother's truck pulling the borrowed horsebox up to the stable, the crunching of the tires on the gravel and the purr of the truck's engine breaking the silence of the waning night. Patrick was waiting at the stable door.

"It's not the fanciest horsebox but it will get us there. Wattrelos isn't far," Maddie said as she climbed out of the truck, leaving it running.

"It be fine," Patrick said. "I have Fionn ready. I wrapped his legs so we won't risk an injury."

"Good. Let's get him and get out of here before anyone sees us."

"I be afraid ye be too late fer that."

Patrick and Maddie froze. From around the side of the barn, Darren Murphy and the stranger he'd met in Lille stepped out of the darkness.

Patrick was the first to find his voice. "Mr. Murphy! What be ye doin' here?"

"I intend to move Fionn this morning. I didn't realize ye would be so helpful. I see ye have the hearse ready ta go."

"I'll not let ye take him again," Patrick said, lifting his chest and rising to his full height, though still far shorter than either man.

"Ye can't stop us," Murphy said, motioning his accomplice forward.

The man, much larger and broader than Patrick *or* Murphy, stepped forward and pulled out a gun.

Maddie let out a whimper. Patrick stiffened.

"Ye see, ye be outnumbered, so to speak," Murphy said with a chuckle. "Now, young lassie, turn off that motor. I brought me own transportation."

Maddie glanced over at Patrick. He nodded and she did as commanded.

"The two of ye follow me," Murphy said as he led them into the barn and to the tack room. "I need to keep ye out of me hair 'til I get a long way away from here."

"Where be ye takin' Fionn?" Patrick said, his voice weak and filled with pleading.

"Somewhere ye will never find him," Murphy said as he shoved Patrick and Maddie into the room. Before shutting and locking the door, he added. "Ye needn't worry 'bout Fionn. I not be a cruel man. He will be well cared for. After all, he only be valuable to us if he be alive and doin' his job."

Murphy paused and pressed his fists against his hips. "If ye really want him to be safe, you'll not go to the police. If ye do, all evidence will have to disappear, if ye get me meaning."

The door slammed shut and a lock clicked into place. Patrick and Maddie were trapped in the windowless room filled with saddles, bridles, and tack trunks. As they stood in the dark, they heard the rhythmic clip-clop of hoofbeats on the cobblestone pavers in the aisle beyond the door.

Maddie ran her hands along the wall until she found the light switch. Filling the room with light did little to dispel the gloom each felt.

"What are we going to do?" Maddie said, her voice shaking. She dropped her head in her hands.

"First, we need ta get out o' here," Patrick said with determination. He stepped to the door and started shaking the doorknob and pounding on the door.

"It's locked. We're stuck," Maddie said dejectedly.

Stepping back and examining the door, Patrick had an idea. "Can ye find me a screwdriver?"

Maddie pursed her lips and knotted her eyebrows. "I know where one is out there," she said, motioning to the door. "But in here, though, we just have tack and grooming supplies." But then she lifted a finger. "Wait, I have an idea!" She ran across the room to a tack trunk and threw open the lid. She shuffled through the brushes and curry combs until she found what she was looking for.

Holding up a hoof pick, she smiled and said, "Will this work?"

"That be perfect," Patrick said, grabbing the metal pick out of her hand. One by one, Patrick used the flat edge of the hoof pick to slowly work the bolts in the door hinges up and out. When the last bolt fell to the floor, Maddie clapped her hands with approval and said, in relief, "You did it!" With the pins removed, Patrick had an easy time pulling the door off the hinges and sliding it away from the lock.

Rushing out of the tack room, Patrick's first thought was of Fionn. Looking down the center aisle of the barn, his heart sank at the sight of Fionn's stall door standing open, the stall empty. It was a sight he had seen once before at Far and Away Farm – a sight he had hoped to never see again. But here he was, faced with the same problem – Where was Fionn?

Chapter 30

Maddie stepped up beside him and put an arm around his waist. "I'm so sorry," she said, a tear rolling down her cheek as she tilted her head against his shoulder.

Patrick shook his head. "Ye did yer best. We were just a wee bit too late."

The two stood in silence for several minutes, each lost in their own thoughts. Maddie was the first to speak.

"On the day Fionn arrived, I heard Murphy tell Monsieur Beaufoy, our barn owner, that they would be moving Fionn as soon as the horse's owner had readied his new farm."

Patrick turned and looked at Maddie. "We need to find the name of the owner he be referrin' to. But how can . . .?"

Raising her eyebrows and holding up her palm, Maddie stopped him in mid-sentence. "My boss said Fionn's board was paid in full. He only takes payment by check. What if he still has that check in his office?"

They both dashed out of the stallion stable and ran into the main barn where the owner of Westwind Farm had his office. Westwind Farm was coming alive for the day. Several stable hands were setting about completing their chores. Buckets of grain and bags of hay were distributed to the horses. Those mares and geldings that had not been fed yet were either stomping or whinnying their impatience.

Maddie stopped one of the barn hands. "*Al-behr*," she began, evoking the French pronunciation of his name, "when you arrived this morning did you see a horsebox leaving the grounds?"

"*Oui, mademoiselle*. It was quite a fancy rig. That is why I noticed it," said the friendly stable hand while leaning on his manure fork.

"Did ye notice which way it went?" Patrick asked.

Albert looked over at the stranger with the odd Irish lilt. His friendly demeanor vanished. He carefully eyed Patrick before answering. "*Non*. I had my mind on my job. I can't be bothered with keeping track of all the comings and goings at this busy farm."

"I understand what ye mean," Patrick said with a chuckle, trying to get on the man's good side. "Thank ye for the help."

Albert turned without responding and continued mucking out a stall.

"Oh, one more thing, Al-behr," Maddie said.

"*Oui, mademoiselle?*" he said, his smile returning as he turned back to look at Maddie.

"Has Monsieur Beaufoy arrived yet?"

"*Non.* He is out of town looking at a new horse to buy for his daughter."

"*Merci.* I'll have to talk to him later, I guess," Maddie added while secretively punching Patrick on his thigh. "We'll just go in his office and leave him a note."

"He'll see it when he returns tomorrow," Albert said. The stable hand returned to his work.

Maddie and Patrick exchanged glances and Maddie winked and smiled. They walked to the front of the long barn and entered the office. Patrick closed the door quietly behind them. He turned to examine the room.

Monsieur Beaufoy kept a neat and tidy office. His desk was absent clutter. The shelves displaying carefully arranged trophies and pictures of horses were free of dust. On the walls hung framed collections of rosettes from numerous victories at horse shows. The file drawers were all closed and, upon examination, organized alphabetically.

Looking into one of the drawers Patrick said, "Where would he file a check?"

"Banking? Boarders? Bills? I don't know," Maddie said, her fingers floating over the file tabs in another drawer.

Files were labeled with all the expected categories — vet bills, hay providers, show forms, memberships, dressage tests — just as one would expect at a show barn. By the fourth drawer, Patrick was about to give up. Just as the discouragement was about to overcome him, he turned around and saw a lone file sitting on a side table. Curious, he went over and picked it up. "Checks to be deposited" was written in bold letters across the front.

"This be it," he exclaimed. "I found it!"

Maddie hurried over as Patrick set the file down on the desk.

"Now let us hope he didn't have time to go to the bank after Murphy was here," Patrick said, rubbing the back of his neck. His hands felt sweaty as he opened the folder. "Will ye recognize a strange name?" he asked, looking over at Maddie.

"I'm sure I will. I know all the boarders and students. Any new name has got to be the one we're looking for." Picking up the top check she said, "We're in luck. The date on this check is from two weeks ago. That means he hasn't been to the bank since Fionn arrived. "

Pursing her lips in concentration, Maddie examined each check. As she recognized the names, she set them to the side. Patrick stood beside her, picking at a fingernail. He closed his eyes and took a deep breath, trying to calm himself.

She was nearly to the bottom of the pile when Maddie stopped. She lifted the check in her hand closer to her face to examine it. Then she gasped and dropped the check. Her hand flew to her throat as she said in a shaky, halting voice, "I can't believe it."

Patrick's eyes shot open. He reached down and snatched the check off the desk. He brought it up to eye-level and read the name. A dazed look crossed his face as he stared at the name on the check.

Chapter 31

A wealthy gentleman in an expensive suit left Charles de Gaulle International Airport in Paris in the comfortable back seat of a chauffeured luxury car. His handsome, cleanshaven face was covered with a smirk as he thought of his newly acquired possession – the greatest racehorse perhaps of all time. True, just as stolen paintings by the great masters had to be kept in sealed chambers, his possession of Fionn would have to be kept a secret from the world.

He hoped the little trick he had arranged in Ireland would stop the hunt. Fionn was an important component in his plan to become the greatest Thoroughbred racing breeder in not only Europe but in all the world. True, the crown princes from the Middle East, with all their oil wealth, were getting into the game, big-time. But with a horse such as Fionn, he would have the edge over them as well.

During the fast-approaching early spring breeding season, he planned to breed Fionn to the twelve incredible mares he had collected over the last few years. His plan was to falsify the pedigrees using the name of one of his other stallions. Once this generation of Fionn's foals made names for themselves as two- and three-year-olds, the money would start rolling in. After retirement, the colts would bring in large amounts as studs. Yes, that was a few years away, but one had to be patient to succeed in this business.

Yes, business. For him it wasn't about the love of the animal — it was about what the animal could do for him. Wealth and prestige were on the line . . . and revenge.

He rubbed his plump hands together in glee. He would get back at those who had denied him in the past. No longer would they have the upper hand. The promise of a bright future turned his smirk to a smile.

The car traveled at high speeds northeast toward the town of Saint Quentin.

Chapter 32

Patrick paced back and forth across Martin Beaufoy's office. He brushed his hands through his curly, red hair as he struggled to accept what he had just learned. "I can't believe an Irishman would do this," he said as he stopped in front of the window. Beyond the barn, he watched as the grooms led horses to their paddocks for daily turnout.

Maddie stepped up beside him. "We can't know what is in people's minds."

"But Irishmen be horse-lovers!"

"Maybe some people love money or fame more than horses."

"I can't believe that," Patrick scoffed.

"Regardless of his motivation, we need to find out where he has purchased a farm. That is where he is taking Fionn."

"I want ta talk to Sir Gallagher. He might have some connections that can help us," Patrick said.

Maddie went to the desk, picked up the receiver, and held it out to Patrick. "I'll cover the cost," she said with a look of both compassion and determination on her face.

Patrick drummed his fingers on the desk as he listened to the phone ringing. He rolled his eyes and was just dropping the receiver when he heard, "Hello?"

Grasping the receiver, he lifted it to his ear. "Sir Gallagher?"

"Yeah."

"It be Patrick."

"Patrick, where be ye? Yer mother said ye went to France."

"Yes, I'm sorry I didn't tell ye. I left in a bit of a rush," Patrick said, wiping the perspiration off his brow. "But I have something very important to tell ye."

"And what might that be?"

"I have found Fionn."

There was silence on the other end for much too long.

"Did ye hear what I said?" Patrick asked, his heart pounding.

"I heard ye. But that be impossible. The Garda just reported to me that they found the charred bones of a hearse in a fire pit in County Leitrim. An anonymous tipster told them Fionn had been taken up there. They searched the entire county and found the bones in a pit located on a deserted farm. They are sure it be Fionn. The Garda has closed the case, convinced it all be over." Bran Gallagher's voice reflected the pain and sorrow he was feeling.

"It can't be Fionn," Patrick said. "I have seen him here in France."

"Where?. . . How? . . . Are ye sure?" Sir Gallagher stammered. "Everyone here is sure the remains be Fionn's. The owner has already made a claim on his insurance policy. He had Fionn insured for 40 million pounds."

Patrick took in a quick intake of breath. "Wow. That be a lot of money."

"Well, Fionn was worth it and possibly much more if he'd had a long career as a stud."

Patrick shook his head, trying to make sense of this unexpected news. But convinced that Fionn was in France, he relayed all that he had done in his search for the stallion. He finished with the involvement of Darren Murphy and the identity of the person who signed the check he even now held in his hand.

"The man who wrote this check for Fionn's board be none other than William Carroll."

Patrick heard Gallagher suck in a quick breath of air. "I be shocked," Sir Gallagher said. "I don't know what ta say. I want, with all me heart, to believe that Fionn is alive, but it seems so impossible that those men could be involved."

Patrick could hear him breathing hard over the phone.

"And ye be sure it be Fionn?" Gallagher said, his voice quiet and quivering.

"I *know* it be Fionn," Patrick said, keeping his voice low but firm.

Gallagher was quiet for quite a while. Finally, he said, "That certainly changes everything." Another pause followed. Then Gallagher said,

"Where be Fionn now? And how will we get him home?"

"I don't know where he be," Patrick said. Suddenly feeling very tired, he sat down in the desk chair. "Murphy and some big thug took him after lockin' Maddie and me in a room."

"He what?" Gallagher exclaimed. "What has come over the man?"

"I can't answer that. But the reason I be callin' is that I need yer help finding where they have taken Fionn."

"What would ye like me to do?"

"Somewhere in France, a horse farm has been purchased . . . probably for a high price. This is where Fionn will be hidden. I need ye to check with yer trainer friends and everyone connected ta either Murphy or Carroll ta see if any o' them have heard anything that will help me."

Chapter 33

Darren Murphy and his unpleasant companion drove south on a maze of small country roads, moving slowly toward the ancient town of Saint Quentin.

The town had seen its share of difficulties from its glory days as the producer of fine wool and batiste fabrics. Both World War I and World War II had left their scars on the town, and the population decreased as manufacturing made a hasty escape. Even the once-prosperous farms in the area had seen better days. But one property, well hidden behind a shield of thick, closely planted trees, had recently sold for a price far above its perceived market value on the condition that the terms of the sale be kept confidential. Of course, that only made the townspeople more curious.

Murphy's companion said very little as he drove, concentrating on towing the horsebox. When Murphy asked him questions, he merely shrugged his shoulders or grunted an unintelligible reply. Murphy, convinced the man wasn't smart enough to put his pants on the right way, kept trying. All Murphy could get out of him was that he represented both the IRA and the buyer in the negotiations for Fionn's kidnapping, and it was his job to see the deal through to completion.

The wrinkled piece of paper on which were scribbled directions to the new farm sat on the dashboard of the truck. They hit a bump in the road and the paper fluttered to the floor. At the same time, the trailer shook the truck in response to Fionn struggling to keep on his feet.

"Watch the road, lad," Murphy said, irritation lacing his speech.

"Dang French canny keep up wit da potholes," the man growled.

"Be that as it may, I don't want ye throwin' the hearse around back there."

The two men drove through the town of Saint Quentin. It was hard for Murphy not to notice the beautiful art deco architecture of many of the buildings. The town had been so destroyed during World War I that many of the town's buildings had been rebuilt in the newly popular style of the time. The Basilique De Saint Quentin, on the other hand, originally built between the twelfth and sixteenth centuries, was reconstructed to look like the original cathedral.

They passed through the town and out the western side, crossing over the river Scheldt as it flowed through the Canal de Saint-Quentin on its way to the North Sea. The land on which the town was built was quite flat, as was the surrounding farmland and patches of thick forest. Murphy understood why this area would make a wonderful horse farm.

Grabbing the handwritten directions, he started looking for the landmarks. After several left and right turns, they came upon a thick row of trees growing along the side of the road. Dense underbrush and intertwining branches prevented any light from entering the forest that bordered the narrow country road. Seeing beyond the forest was an impossibility.

The wall of trees extended for nearly a mile. In the middle of the expanse of foreboding forest a copper gate, oxidized to a pale green and covered with curling vines, stood beside the road. Beyond the gate, a narrow lane disappeared into the darkness.

"That be it," Murphy said.

His companion grunted and put his foot on the brake. "Ye sure? This don't look like any hearse farm I ever seen. I don't want ta be takin' any wrong turns and gettin' meself stuck where I canny turn 'round."

"This be it. I be sure," Murphy said with a huff, tired of having to explain himself to this man whom Murphy viewed as nothing but an undesirable criminal. To Murphy the man could best be described by the Irish term of a "melter," a person who is a bit stupid, or at least very annoying.

The driver stopped the truck and horsebox in front of the gate. Murphy climbed out of the cab of the truck. The gate was locked. Using the combination code he was given, he lifted the paddle lock and spun the dial. It snapped open. Removing the lock, he pushed the gate to one side. It creaked on its heavy hinges as it swung open.

They followed the long drive through the dense forest. Nearly a quarter of a mile down the lane, the forest opened revealing fenced paddocks and numerous structures. Murphy's eyes opened wide, and he sat back in his seat. From the road, it was impossible to tell that such an estate existed.

The farm to which they were taking Fionn had once been an elegant establishment. Built by a wealthy member of French Royalty, the chateau was built in the classic Tudor style. It was a large, three-story home with a brick exterior featuring large portions of white stucco and decorative half-timbering. The home had a romantic and slightly medieval appearance.

To one side was the stable, built in the same style with brick, white stucco, and exposed timbers. No expense had been spared in the original construction, nor in the recent restoration.

Murphy jumped out of the truck as soon as it came to a stop. "I'll be gettin' the hearse," he called over his shoulder.

With the sun sitting on the horizon, streaks of pink and blue painted the western sky. Once Fionn was backed out of the horsebox, the stallion stopped and looked up, as though appreciating the beauty of the sunset.

"Let's be walkin', lad," Murphy said, giving a slight tug on the lead.

Fionn dropped his head and followed as they walked past the main barn to a smaller stable nestled near the forest. Fionn was hidden away in the back of the stable just as a luxury car pulled up the long drive and stopped at the Tudor chateau.

Chapter 34

For the next few days after his first call to Sir Gallagher, placed on the day Fionn disappeared for the second time, Patrick tried to keep himself busy helping Maddie at Westwind Farm. Just being with horses kept his jittery mind at ease and helped lower his anxiety. Not only did the horses help calm him, he knew the importance of transmitting a sense of peace and well-being to the horses themselves. In turn, the positive energy emitted by horses when one is around them eventually gets through the hard human shell. And there is something to be said for plain old physical labor to help one focus on something other than one's troubles.

At last, Patrick found himself humming while he worked.

The two young adults returned to Maddie's parents' home in the evening for a dinner of wonderful French cooking provided by Maddie's mother. Looking forward to the nightly feast helped give Patrick something else to think about as well.

Each night, Patrick called Sir Gallagher.

"It be Patrick," he said as soon as Gallagher answered the phone.

"Yes, lad. Me thought as much. I still have not news for ye. Our Irishman appears to be out of the country, but that be not unusual fer him. Neither his closest friends nor his staff know where he has gone or when he'll be back. They all know nothing about a farm somewhere in France."

Each night the answer was the same, and Patrick's heart felt heavier and heavier every time he hung up the receiver.

On the third night, after yet another disappointing call, Patrick joined Maddie's family for dinner.

They passed him a bowl filled with chunks of duck meat, beans, carrots, onions, and breadcrumbs. The aromatic spices used for seasoning caused Patrick's mouth to water and lifted his spirits slightly. He took his first bite, closed his eyes, and savored the unique blend of flavors.

"This be delicious, Madame Segard."

Maddie's mother smiled. "*Merci beaucoup!*" she said, her face beaming and her eyes sparkling. "It's fun to cook for someone who appreciates my creations, even if it is something as common as *cassoulet*. I thought on such a cold February night, you'd appreciate some French comfort food."

Just as Patrick was breaking his baguette, the phone on the wall rang, interrupting the cordial conversation going on around the table. Maddie's father got up to answer it.

"*Qui,* he is right here."

Patrick looked up, cocking his head. "For me?"

Monsieur Segard nodded and extended his hand holding the phone toward Patrick.

Patrick's heart jumped to his throat. *Could it be Sir Gallagher with some unexpected news?* He dared not hope.

"Sir Gallagher?" Patrick said, his voice shaking.

A jovial laugh crossed over the phone lines. "I be afraid not, but I be just as good if not better!"

"Ronan!" Patrick exclaimed in genuine surprise. "Why be ye callin'?"

"I've news for ye, but I want to tell ye in person."

"Ach. Tell me now. I could use some good news."

"Not now, laddie. I want to make sure ye'll pick me up from the train station."

"Ye be comin' here?"

"I am, of course. I want to see beautiful Maddie. Ye don't get to keep her for yerself, ye know!"

"When will ye be here?"

"I be here now. Come get me!"

Chapter 35

While Patrick and Maddie worked at Westwind farm and hoped for information, the Tudor chateau outside Saint Quentin was a buzz of activity. During his first day on the farm, William Carroll put out a call for prospective household help and horse-handlers. He placed an ad in the local paper. The word spread quickly through Saint Quentin that jobs were available, and people lined up at the door for a chance to find employment.

As prospective employees stood outside shivering in the wind and rain, Carroll stormed around his office, yelling into the phone.

"I told ye that any ransom ye could get was up to the likes of ye. I paid yer group with the arms as we agreed. It not be my fault they won't pay a ransom. Maybe ye shouldn't have been so greedy."

He paused and listened to the response, his face getting redder by the minute.

"Don't ye go threatin' me. We had an agreement. I pay ye in arms, ye get the hearse out of the country. As far as I be concerned, the contract is completed. Now get yer thug off me property." He slammed down the phone and stormed out of the room.

Murphy and the burly IRA man were drinking tea in the parlor. Murphy was frowning. His colleague was glaring at him. Murphy had not been pleased that his unwanted companion had accompanied him everywhere he went whether in the stable or the house. Both men looked up as the Irishman stormed into the room.

"Murphy, I want ye to move yer family to the chateau and manage the farm. Pick who ye want for help at the house and the barn from the people lined up outside."

Turning to the other man, he said, "And ye. I don't want to see yer face in me presence again. Yer service is no longer needed."

"I canny be leavin' just because ye say so," said the bulky man, his eyes narrowed.

"I be in charge here, and I said *leave*!"

Watching the unnamed man stomp through the front door brought a smile to Murphy's face.

On the evening that Patrick received the call from Ronan, he and Maddie rushed to the train station in Lille to pick up their friend. They saw him standing in front of the station when they pulled up. His smile spread across his face as he waved.

Patrick jumped out of the car and embraced his friend. "This be a surprise! I be so glad to see ye," he said as he took Ronan's bag and put it in the boot.

"How did ye know I be here?" Patrick asked as they climbed into Maddie's car.

"Yer mum told me when I called with news." He reached forward and gave Maddie a squeeze on the shoulder. "How be me best lass?"

Maddie turned and smiled. "It's so wonderful to see you, Ronan."

"Enough of the niceties," Patrick said. "What be the news?"

As they drove into Lille, Ronan relayed what he knew.

"Me acquaintance that met with ye, Patrick, is trying to keep abreast of what is happening with Fionn," Ronan began. "It seems the IRA is broken up into several factions and the one responsible for Fionn's disappearance is quite upset. They hoped to collect two million pounds as ransom for the hearse, but the owner has refused to pay."

"Yeah," Patrick said. "I be aware of that."

"Well, it appears the ransom was not the sole purpose of the kidnapping."

"They were hired in exchange for a payment in arms and ammunition," Patrick said.

"Oh, so ye knew that did ye? But they had hoped to double dip – the arms payment *and* a ransom payment." Ronan paused and looked out the window. "Charming, this place ye call home, Maddie."

"Thank you," she said watching the road as the windshield wipers swished back and forth.

"What be I sayin'?" Ronan said, unzipping his jacket.

"Nothing we hadn't figured out already," Patrick said.

"Well, obviously ye discovered that Fionn was shipped to France or ye wouldn't be here."

"True," said Patrick with a chuckle.

"But where in France? Do ye know that?"

"He was at a farm not far from Lille – a farm where Maddie works. I saw him."

"Ye saw him and ye let him get away?" Ronan said, his voice filled with astonishment.

"You would have, too, if you'd seen the size of the gun and the monster wielding it," Maddie said over her shoulder.

"Ach. I guess so," Ronan said. "But for the good news, me contact knows where he be now."

Chapter 36

The next morning, Maddie's two friends helped complete her chores at Westwind Farm, then they all climbed in her car and drove to Saint Quentin. They traveled south beneath the lowered French sky as the clouds temporarily held onto their raindrops.

Arriving at noon, the peal of the thirty-seven bells atop the grand building that housed property records called to them. The large *L'hôtel de ville* of Saint-Quentin (the City Hall) was originally created in the Gothic style but was one of the buildings severely damaged in the First World War. When it was restored in 1926, it was modified in the Art Déco style, as were many of the buildings.

After finding a parking spot along a narrow side street, Maddie led the way to the front of the magnificent building.

They walked into the cavernous foyer, their footsteps echoing off the walls and high ceiling. Patrick and Ronan looked around with mouths dropping open. Maddie, accustomed to the grandeur of French buildings, approached a man dressed in a policeman's uniform. His badge sparkled from where it was pinned on his chest.

"*Qui, mademoiselle?*" he said with a friendly smile.

"We are curious about recent property sales. Is there a record of those held here in city hall?" she said, giving the man her best smile in return.

He nodded and pointed the way to the Records Department.

For the next hour Patrick, Maddie, and Ronan combed through the records of all real estate transactions in and around Saint Quentin, searching for the name of the Irishman William Carroll they believed purchased a farm in the area. Working backwards from the most recent, they finally reached the dates for October, five months previous.

"Look at this, will ye?" Ronan said, stepping back and pointing at the book in front of him. "There be a page missing. It jumps from October sixteenth to October eighteenth."

Patrick and Maddie looked around him and peered at the pages. Flipping them back and forth with knitted brows, they pursed their lips.

"Could it be that no one made a transaction on that day?" Maddie proposed.

"Could be. But considering all the other business days have records on them, that seems odd," Ronan said.

"Go talk to the receptionist. Maybe she knows," Patrick suggested.

As the only one of the three who spoke the language of France, bilingual Maddie went up to the desk behind which a tall, thin woman dressed all in black was working over some papers. Maddie cleared her throat and the woman looked up, peering through her thick glasses.

"*Oui?*" the woman behind the desk said.

"We noticed what appears to be a missing record for October seventeenth of last year. Do you know what could have happened to it?" Maddie asked in her lovely native language.

The woman stood abruptly and walked over to the table where the two boys still stood with the notebooks open. *"Pardon em moi,"* she said as she pushed them aside and reached out for the book. Flipping the pages back and forth, she sighed.

Speaking to Maddie, she said, "It does appear to be missing; you are certainly right there," she said. "I'm sorry, but I can't explain it." Closing the book with a bang, she turned to Maddie. She paused for a moment as she examined the young woman closely. Then she inquired, "Where are you staying? I'll check some other sources and get back to you."

Maddie gave her the information of a youth hostel they were planning to check into, and they took their leave, thanking her profusely. *"Merci beaucoup,"* Maddie said.

Once outside, Ronan, rubbing his stomach, said, "I be starvin'. I need some o' that famous French comfort food."

Maddie led them to the nearest bistro, just around the block from City Hall. They settled in at a round table in the back corner. The table was partially hidden by some large palms set in colorful pots and placed close together. They took off their coats, enjoying the warmth in the bistro. Delicious smells emanated from the kitchen.

Maddie guided them through the menu until each made their selection. Hot soup and succulent sandwiches arrived quickly.

As they were eating, a man and a woman seated themselves on the other side of the palms from where the three friends were eating their lunch. Maddie's back was to the potted plants, but she could hear their conversation. She shushed Patrick and Ronan and leaned back to listen. Her two friends held their breath, curious as to what Maddie was hearing. They, too, tried to catch the conversation but understood very little of the French being spoken.

"*Qui*. It was just three kids, nineteen or twenty at the oldest," said the woman whose voice Maddie recognized as belonging to the clerk in the records room.

"What were they looking for?" said the man.

"I can't be sure, but they noticed the missing page from October."

"Wait. Tell me what these kids looked like."

"There was a beautiful girl with long dark hair and big eyes. I didn't pay a lot of attention to the young men, but one was short with curly red hair."

"Patrick McCallin. I'd bet my life," said the man. "If it is, he's looking for Fionn. What did you tell them?"

"Nothing. Nothing at all," the woman said, rubbing her clammy palms on her skirt. "I did get the name of the youth hostel where they are staying."

"Which one?" the man interrupted impatiently.

"*Le Parc*, just a few streets up."

"Good. I'll take it from here. If they come back, just say there is no sign of a record for that day."

Chapter 37

Patrick, Ronan, and Maddie sat frozen in place. Maddie looked from one to the other and put her finger to her lips. No one said a word. They waited until the two people on the other side of the palms stood to leave. Patrick dropped his chin and shielded his face with his hand. He peeked through his eyelashes and watched them as they turned, giving him just a moment to catch a glimpse of their faces. The woman was the clerk they had just met at City Hall. The man was tall, and thin, and had a black goatee. His black hair was slicked back from his forehead. He was no one Patrick remembered having seen before.

Once the two were out the door, Patrick leaned across the table. "What be that all about?" Patrick whispered.

"I recognized the woman as the clerk in City Hall," said Ronan.

"Something very suspicious is going on," Maddie said. "They know something about the property sale."

"Or, perhaps the man is involved in the purchase himself," Ronan said.

"And . . . ?" Patrick prodded.

"They are keeping the records a secret," Maddie said.

"But why would they be trying to keep it secret?" Patrick asked, his eyebrows raised.

"They want to hide the name of the person who purchased the property," said Maddie.

"But why would the clerk go along with that?" asked Patrick.

"She be either paid off or threatened to remain silent ta hide the purchase," Ronan said. "Either she be afraid, or she fears losing the money she has been bribed with. We'll never get any information out o' that woman. We be goin' to have to find some other way ta locate the farm."

Maddie raised her eyebrows as she lifted a finger. "Horse farms need to hire help."

"That be a good point," said Patrick.

"If you were looking for help to run a horse farm," Maddie said, "where would you start?"

"I'd put an ad in the newspaper," said Ronan.

"I'd go talk to other farms or tack and feed stores," said Patrick.

"Ok. Which one should we do first?"

"The newspaper," Patrick and Ronan said in unison.

The local paper was called *L'Union* and was located right in the middle of town at 10 Henri Martin Boulevard. Their office was in a quaint building that was once a bakery. Its large front windows revealed printing presses and rolls of paper. Newspaper men and women were hustling around. It was a busy place as the staff worked to get out the latest edition.

When Maddie opened the front door, a little bell rang, too softly for anyone to hear over the din of the presses. A short, thin, balding man, the sleeves of his white shirt rolled up past his elbows, noticed their arrival and stepped up to the counter to greet them.

"*Bonjour,*" he said with a smile. "What can I do for you today?"

Patrick stepped forward. "Does your paper have a help wanted section?"

"But of course. May I show you our latest edition?"

"Thank you," Patrick said.

"I must add, however, that we only print our paper in French."

Both boys looked at Maddie.

"*Qui,*" she said, her dark hair and eyes clearly charming the journalist. "I can help with that."

"*Qui,* mademoiselle, I would be happy to be of help," he said as he smiled at Maddie.

With yesterday's paper spread out across a table, Maddie thumbed through the pages. In the back section she found the help wanted ads. Starting at the top, she ran her finger down the columns as she read about requests for bistro workers, office clerical positions, used car salesmen, nannies, and on and on. But there was nothing about stable hands.

Patrick watched her, his eyes hopeful, but his heart dropping with every ad passed by.

Maddie got to the end and looked up at Patrick and Ronan. Shaking her head she said, "There's nothing here that can help us."

"Maybe we should check an older edition," suggested Patrick, still clinging to hope.

"We can try," Maddie said, but her voice reflected her skepticism.

The paper from the day before offered nothing. The day before that? Nothing again. Three days before? Still nothing. But the paper from four days earlier showed an ad that looked promising.

Help Wanted.
The owner of the
newly restored
Chateau Dubois
is seeking
experienced horse
handlers and
stable hands as
well as household
staff. Interviews
will be conducted
tomorrow morning
at 10 a.m.

Patrick felt his heart skip a beat as a shiver went down his spine. "Chateau Dubois? Could that be the place?"

"I'd bet me life on it," Ronan said, snatching up the paper and doing his best to read the French words in the ad.

"The interviews would have been held three days ago," Maddie added, twirling a strand of hair around her finger, deep in thought. "That would be just about the time Fionn was taken from Westwind."

"And just the time when they would need stable hands," added Patrick.

"Now ta find out where Chateau Dubois be located . . ." Ronan said.

Chapter 38

The staff at *L'Union* proved to be very helpful. Their records of ad sales were up to date and well organized. Fortunately, the man who had filled out the form had included the address of the chateau. The newspaperman gave them basic directions.

Getting back in Maddie's car, the three sleuths drove west, through the town and over the river Scheldt.

"We need to keep following this road until we see a junction," Maddie said, reminding the boys of the directions they had been given. "Then we take the narrow country road going to the left."

"And ye said something about a thick stand o' trees," Patrick reminded her.

"Yes. The uncleared forest land will be on our left. He said it hid the chateau from view."

"Then how will we know when we be there?" Ronan asked.

"He said to watch for a copper gate," Maddie said.

"We best be findin' it before the sun goes down," added Patrick.

There were a variety of farms on either side of the road. Some looked prosperous and well-cared-for. Others seemed to have deteriorated with neglect. In some fields, horses grazed contentedly. Other fields held cattle or goats. Still other fields had been overtaken with weeds and brush while metal farm implements lay abandoned and rusting.

The farmhouses reflected the same variation in care and attention. Some homes were neat and tidy with outbuildings to match. Other properties had homes in need of paint and new roofs. In the worst of the cases, their wooden sides bleached white by the sun, their roofs sagging, signaled homes deserted since the war.

But, in all, the countryside around Saint Quentin was fertile and cultivated.

Turning left at the junction they had been told to watch for brought them alongside a thick forest that appeared to have been there since the dark ages, unusual for the area that was otherwise covered with cleared farmland. The forest made for an early twilight. Shadows darkened the road, the dense forest pulling a black curtain between the road and the lowering sun. The darkness caused Maddie to drive right past the gate. She realized they had missed it only when they arrived at the clear rolling hills of another farm. Shaking her head, she let out a breath. "I thought you two were watching. I'll need to turn around. It must be back there somewhere."

"Sorry, Maddie," Patrick said. "I guess me eyes didn't adjust to the dark."

Maddie found a wide area beside the road and turned around. This time, she drove slowly once they entered the forest. The thick trees and dense underbrush had a chilling effect on all of them. Patrick unbuttoned the top of his shirt and rubbed his neck. He stared into the foreboding woods as he bit his lower lip, searching for an entrance.

Halfway down the stretch of forest, Ronan called out, "There it be. I see it!"

Maddie slammed on the brakes, throwing them all forward. The Renault stopped in front of an ornate copper gate set back several meters from the road. Once beautiful and well maintained, the structure was now aged and overgrown with vines and latched securely with a paddle lock and chain.

Silence filled the car and fear filled their hearts as they each stared at the gate.

At last, Patrick spoke, his voice but a whisper. "This be it. This be where they be hidin' Fionn. I know it, deep in me bones."

"I feel it, too," added Maddie.

"Not me. It just gives me the creeps," said Ronan.

Patrick got out of the car. Placing his hands on his hips, he examined the gate more closely. The gate was secured tightly, making access to the road impossible. He couldn't even squeeze his small body through. However, as he looked from one side to the other, he noticed that there was no fencing extending beyond the pillars that supported the gate. It was only the dense forest with its thick tree trunks and wild underbrush that formed the barrier along the road. He dashed back to the car.

"We can get there through the forest," he said.

"Be ye sure?" Ronan asked.

"Non. I can't be sure until we work our way around the gates and through the woods."

"Being that it is now so dark," Maddie said, motioning toward the night sky with her hands, "I suggest we go back to the hostel, make a plan, and get better prepared for whatever we decide to do."

Pushing aside his disappointment at being so close and having to turn away, Patrick could see the wisdom in what she was saying. After all, these were dangerous men they were dealing with. He didn't want to put himself, his friends, or his horse in a perilous situation. Shrugging his shoulders, he climbed back in the car.

They had just started moving north when a car passed them. Patrick stared out the back window as the car slowed and turned into the drive by the gate. A man got out, approached the gate, and opened it. When he turned around, the headlights illuminated his face.

His heart pounding, Patrick whipped around. "I be right. That be Darren Murphy what just passed us."

"Now we know for sure," Maddie said, her voice cold as she hit her fist against the steering wheel. "That is where Fionn is being hidden."

Chapter 39

Le Parc Youth Hostel was located in a tall, narrow building pressed between several other townhomes. The red brick façade was garnished with a welcoming deep green door, making it stand out from the other homes that lined the street. Located in the center of town, it was the perfect location for tourists wanting to experience the true Saint Quentin vibe.

Parking along the street, Patrick, Ronan, and Maddie grabbed their backpacks out of the boot and hurried down the cobblestone road to the front door, eager to get to their rooms and start planning.

They entered the front room and approached the check-in desk.

"*Bonsoir*, Good evening," greeted the short, plump woman with graying hair and friendly smile as they approached. "Do you have reservations?"

"Non. We need three rooms, please," said Patrick as he pulled his wallet out of the front pocket of his backpack.

"Name please?" she said, her eyes twinkling.

"Patrick McCallin."

"Her eyes opened wide. Oh, Monsieur McCallin, I have been expecting you. A gentleman left a message for you. I set it right here on my desk. Let me find it." She turned and shuffled through some papers on the desk. "Ah, here it is," she said, lifting a small envelope and returning to the counter. She handed the letter to Patrick who took it with knitted brow and pursed lips.

"Who be it from?" asked Ronan.

"I haven't a blady notion," Patrick said as he flipped the envelope over and back. "The only thing it says on the outside is me name."

"Open it," prodded Ronan.

"I'll open it when we be in our rooms."

"Here are your room keys," the kindly mistress of the house said. "Your rooms are on the third floor. The bathroom is at the end of the hall. Please enjoy your stay."

Patrick and his friends each took a key. Ronan and Maddie hurried up the stairs. Before following them out of the lobby, Patrick turned back and addressed their hostess.

"Might ye have a piece of stationary?"

"*Qui,* Of course," she said with a smile. She handed him a small white piece of paper and an envelope with the address of the Le Parc Youth Hostel in the corner.

Patrick scribbled a quick note on the paper, folded it, and inserted it in the envelope. After writing an address on the front, he handed it back to the mistress. The envelope was addressed to Sir Bran Gallagher. "Please post this for me," he said.

"Of course, I'll put it in this evening's pick-up," she said with a smile. "It will go out tonight."

Ronan and Maddie entered their respective rooms, dropped their packs on their beds, and rushed out to find Patrick.

Patrick entered his room clutching the note he had been given. His mind was racing, attempting to figure out who might have sent him a message.

"Open it," said Maddie as she entered Patrick's room.

Patrick set his pack on the bed and sat down beside it. He inserted his finger in the flap of the envelope, ripped it open, and pulled out a small notecard. Turning it over he read the handwritten message:

> If you know what's good for you, you will go back to Ireland and forget about Fionn.

Patrick's brow furrowed and his hands shook. He read it again.

"Well, what does it say?" Maddie asked.

Patrick looked up and extended his hand holding the note. Maddie snatched it away and read it. Her eyes opened wide, and her chin dropped. She handed the note to Ronan whose response was similar.

"It's a threat," Maddie said, her voice trembling.

Patrick nodded. "That couldn't be more clear." He wiped the perspiration off his forehead. "Maybe we should do as it says and call this whole thing off."

"What?" Ronan said. "I can't believe ye just said that. In all the time I've known ye, I never saw ye back away from a challenge."

"Well, that would be a four-legged challenge, not a two-legged one," Patrick said, rubbing his hand through his red curls as he thought about the huge gun-wielding man he met at Westwind Farm. "I can handle the four-legged kind of challenge. I don't know about this kind."

"Ye can handle this one, too," Ronan said, patting Patrick on the shoulder. "I know ye can."

Patrick looked up. "Are ye just trying to boost me confidence?"

Ronan smiled. "Aye. Did it work?"

"Naw, not really," Patrick responded with a sigh as he threw himself back on the bed.

Chapter 40

My, my. I didn't expect to see the three of you up so early," said the portly mistress of the hostel, with a smile. "Can I fix you some breakfast?"

"No, thank you," Maddie said as she placed her room key on the counter. "We are checking out."

The little woman's smile disappeared. "Is there something wrong? Were you not happy with the accommodations?"

"Oh, the rooms were lovely," Maddie said. "We have just changed our plans and will be returning home today."

The woman cocked her head. "I hope the message you received was not bad news."

Maddie paused. "Well, not entirely good, I should say."

"Oh, dear. I'm so sorry."

"It can't be helped," Maddie said, looking back at Patrick and Ronan who had just come down the staircase.

Patrick and Ronan placed their keys on the counter.

"I'm sorry to see you leave so soon," the mistress of the hostel said.

Patrick cleared his throat. "Do ye remember what the man looked like that left me this message?" Patrick said, holding up the note.

"Well, he wasn't a Frenchman, to be sure. I could tell by his accent, though he spoke fluent French. Other than that, I didn't notice anything in particular that stood out, other than he was tall and thin, and had a black goatee."

Patrick looked from Maddie to Ronan. *Could it have been the man in the Bistro?* he wondered.

Patrick, Ronan, and Maddie waited until they were out in the street, out of earshot, to discuss what to do next.

"It's clear someone knows why we are here," Maddie said, brushing her long hair out of her face, against the desires of the wind.

"And that someone is deeply involved in Fionn's kidnapping, to be sure," said Patrick.

"And he, whoever he be, isn't afraid to use threats," added Ronan.

"But the question is, how serious are the threats?" asked Maddie.

"I not be sure I want to stick around to find out," said Patrick with a huff.

Ronan gave him a punch on the shoulder. "We already went over that last night. We be in this together, thick or thin."

Patrick set his jaw and clenched his fists, then nodded.

The ninety-minute drive back to Lille was a quiet one. Each was lost in their own thoughts. As Maddie pulled up to her home, she turned off the car and looked over at her friends. "Well, are we still in agreement?"

Patrick nodded; his lips pursed.

"Let's get moving before I change me mind," said Ronan.

Patrick swung around and glared at Ronan. "Now who be the one with the nerves? Where is all that bravado?"

Ronan shrugged his shoulders.

Maddie went into the house to talk to her parents and make a phone call. Patrick and Ronan sat in the car, waiting impatiently.

"Are ye sure we shouldn't just turn this over to the Garda?" Ronan said, his arms folded across his chest.

"Not until we have Fionn safely away from them."

"Well, I sure hope this works," Ronan mumbled.

"Me be with you," Patrick said as he watched Maddie rushing out the front door of her house.

She jumped in the car. "It's all set," she said.

"Then let's be off," Patrick said, trying to calm his nerves and sound confident.

Maddie drove across Lille and into the countryside, heading toward Hem but stopping just short of Westwind Farm. Pulling into a small farm with two horses in the front pasture, Maddie drove up to the farmhouse. "This is my friend's house. I'll be right back with the keys to the truck. Who's going to drive my car?"

"That be me," said Ronan.

Maddie jumped out and Ronan took her place in the driver's seat while she went into the house to get the truck keys. Patrick and Ronan watched her come out of the house and get in an old pickup truck attached to an even older straight-load horsebox.

She pulled up beside the boys and rolled down the window on the truck. "Follow me to Westwind. You can help me clean stalls and bring horses in."

"Anything for ye, gorgeous, be alright with me," Ronan said with a wink of his eye.

She rolled her eyes, shook her head, and waved them off before pulling out of the farm.

Darkness settled like a thick blanket over the forest that housed the chateau. The full moon peeked between the clouds, offering just the slightest illumination as Maddie followed Ronan and Patrick down the dark country road. Both car and truck were driving with headlights off. As Ronan drove, Patrick continually checked out the back window to make sure she was still behind them. They crept down the road, looking for the copper gate. A deer bounded onto the road from the forest, stopping just long enough to look at them before continuing on, only to disappear between the trees on the other side. When the gate came into view, Ronan blinked his lights on and then off. Maddie responded in kind. They continued down the quiet road until they came to the end of the forest. Ronan pulled over to the side of the road. Maddie followed, stopping right behind them.

Patrick and Ronan got out of the car and walked up to Maddie.

"This be where ye wait for us," Patrick said. "We be bringin' Fionn out through the forest. Have the trailer door open."

"I know the plan," Maddie said, chewing on her thumbnail. "Be careful."

"We've got this," Ronan said, forcing a smile and ruffling her black hair.

Maddie swatted his hand away. "You better!"

While Maddie settled in to wait, Patrick and Ronan crossed the road and plunged into the thick forest that grew right up to the road. They soon found themselves tangled in brambles and struggling to work their way around trees and over leafless bushes. Broken branches and exposed roots caused them to take turns stumbling and falling. The wet boughs of the evergreens sent water running down their backs. Wild animals, deer probably, scurried out of their way but offered little guidance on how to negotiate the rough terrain.

Low-hanging branches sliced at Patrick's face, but a few scrapes didn't bother him. His only thoughts were of rescuing Fionn. The going was frustratingly slow, much slower than Patrick expected.

"Whose idea was this?" grumbled Ronan as he pushed a branch out of his face.

"No choice, mate," Patrick said. "But I must admit, I didn't realize it would be this hard."

"Well, we sure as heck canny take Fionn back through this," said Ronan as he ducked under a thick branch and scraped his arm on the trunk of a tree.

"We'll have to bring him back down the drive," Patrick said, sure that his friend was right. "Let's hope we come upon a deer trail." That was not to be.

Thick, slow-moving clouds concealed the moon, and the canopy overhead made for an even darker journey. Only Patrick's keen sense of direction kept them moving toward the estate.

It must have been half an hour before Ronan saw a flash of light glowing between the trees ahead of them.

"I see something up ahead," he said, his height giving him the advantage.

"Where? I don't see it," said Patrick.

Ronan put his finger to his lips. "Sh-h-h. Keep movin'. It just be a short distance away," he whispered.

Both boys began tiptoeing through the brush, trying to avoid being heard.

Shortly thereafter, they arrived at the edge of the forest where it bordered a sweeping, manicured lawn leading up to a beautiful chateau whose outer walls were crawling with densely braided vines. The lights from the large Tudor home glowed from every window, sending patches of gold onto the gardens and grass.

Patrick and Ronan dropped to their bellies and crept to the edge of the lawn, concealed by the thick underbrush.

Patrick's eyes scanned the grounds. He looked over at Ronan, his eyebrows raised. "Impressive," he whispered.

"Just be a wee hovel," Ronan said with a crooked smile.

A moving shadow on his left caught Patrick's attention. He jerked his head around just in time to see a doe and her fawn step out of the forest and begin munching on the lush lawn. Patrick scolded himself for being so jumpy.

Turning his attention back to the chateau, he could see people moving past the windows on the inside of the manor.

Patrick caught his breath as he squinted and peered at the windows. "That looks like the Murphy children," he said, scratching his head.

The sound of car tires on the gravel drive and the rumble of an engine broke the silence of the night. Patrick and Ronan turned their heads in the direction from which the noise was coming. The yellow beam of headlights was seen bouncing in the darkness. The doe and her fawn made a hasty retreat into the forest. Soon a Black BMW appeared out of the forest and moved up to the front of the chateau.

Two men stepped out of the car as Darren Murphy appeared at the front door. The light from the porch lit their faces.

Patrick elbowed Ronan in the ribs. "That's William Carroll," he whispered.

"And the other man, the tall, thin one with the goatee, is the man we saw in the bistro," Ronan responded quietly.

Chapter 41

Patrick and Ronan remained on their stomachs, hidden beneath the brush, watching the activity in the manor. Slowly, the lights began to dim as the inhabitants retired for the night.

Patrick felt collywobbles coming on. He took a few deep breaths to calm himself. "Remind me that we can do this," he whispered.

"No problem, mate," Ronan whispered back. "Just follow the plan. We sneak into the barn, put Fionn's headstall over his head, snap on the lead, and take him out the door."

"Easy as me mother's banoffee pie."

"That's right. And don't ye forget it," Ronan said with a chuckle.

The forest sounds increased as all activity in the chateau ceased. Patrick watched the hour hand on his watch move one complete revolution. The hair on the back of his neck stood on end and a shiver went through his body. He took a deep breath and let it out slowly. "It be time," he said.

Ronan said nothing as he crawled out from under the brush and stood on the manicured lawn. Patrick followed.

Both young men hunched over and slowly crept along the edge of the forest, hidden by the darkness and the cold drizzle coming from the low clouds. They kept glancing over at the house to make sure everyone was still asleep. They arrived at the gravel drive, paused, and looked both ways.

"The coast is clear," said Patrick. They hurried across the gravel road, their feet crunching on the rocks as they ran.

Just as they reached the shelter of the trees on the far side of the road, they heard a dog barking from inside the house. They ducked behind some tree trunks. Peering through the branches, they noticed a light come on in one of the upper rooms of the house.

Patrick felt his heart start to pound, and he chewed on his lower lip. He watched as a main floor light came back to life and the front door opened. Patrick dug his nails into the bark of the tree, and he held his breath. He recognized Darren Murphy as the man stepped out onto the front porch, holding the collar of the dog. The animal continued to bark.

Patrick and Ronan remained frozen in place.

Murphy looked from side to side. "Hush boy," he said to quiet the dog. "It be nothin' ta worry 'bout." Turning back into the house, he added: "Back ta bed with ye."

Ronan blew out the breath he had been holding. "That be a close call," he said.

Patrick and Ronan stayed in their hiding place until the lights went out again. Several minutes later, they stepped out of the forest and worked their way toward the barn, this time with greater stealth to avoid arousing the dog again.

They felt their way across the front of the barn until they found a door. Sliding it open, they stepped inside. No lights were on in the stable and they decided to keep it that way so as not to call attention to themselves.

The munching sounds of horses eating hay along with the occasional stomp of a hoof, told them they were in the right place. The sound of contented horses was both familiar and comforting. Typically, horses only sleep for short periods at a time. So, Patrick was not surprised to find them all eating or shuffling around in their stalls.

Ronan pulled a flashlight from his jacket pocket and switched it on. He shot the beam around the barn. It was a small barn with four large box stalls, probably a stallion barn. Each stall was occupied. Parked in the rear of the aisleway near the solid back wall, was a tractor.

Patrick and Ronan went up to the nearest stall. Inside was a large, chestnut stallion. The stall across from that held a smaller dapple-gray one. Next to the gray was a bay horse that could have passed for Fionn if it had a white blaze and four white socks. Turning around and facing the last stall, Patrick felt his heart thumping in his chest.

"Fionn," he said.

Immediately the sound of rustling straw was heard and a bay horse with a white blaze down his face put his head over the stall door. Traces of the black hair dye were still visible on his face, body, and legs, further evidence that this was Fionn. The stallion released a deep, throaty nicker.

Patrick smiled. "Fionn," he repeated.

He hurried across the aisle and grabbed the head collar hanging by the door. He had just slid the door open when the lights in the barn burst on.

Patrick squinted as he waited for his eyes to adjust to the bright lights. Turning back around, he faced the door. Standing in the doorway were two men, Darren Murphy and William Carroll. Murphy and Carroll both held guns, and they were pointed at Patrick and Ronan.

Patrick gasped, desperate for air. Ronan stood frozen in place.

"Ye just cain't leave well enough alone, can ye," Carroll said. "I warned ye to stay outta this." He shook his head. "Now ye leave me no choice."

"W-what are ye going to do?" stammered Patrick, sweat beading on his forehead.

"I will have to destroy the evidence," Carroll said.

"Fionn? No! You can't do that!" Patrick said, throwing his arms around the horse's neck. He glared at the two men, his jaw clenched as he fought back the tears forming in his eyes.

"As I said, ye leave me no choice. As much as it pains me to lose all the time and money I have invested, it will have to be done."

"The fault be all on ye," said Murphy to Patrick. "If ye hadn't been so intent on acting the maggot, behaving so foolishly, the hearse would have had a wonderful life here in France."

Ronan stepped forward and both men turned their guns toward him. "Stay back if ye know what's good for ye," Murphy said.

Ronan continued forward, his features creased with determination. The butt of Carroll's gun landed squarely in Ronan's stomach with such force the boy tumbled backward, landing with a "humpf" on the brick aisleway.

Ronan folded over, clasping his stomach as he glared up at his attacker. "Ye won't get away with this. . . People know we be here," he gasped out between groans.

"They won't believe two crazy young boys over two well-respected men," said Carroll. "They'll think ye are 'wired to the moon' as we say in Ireland. Ye be crazy."

"We have proof that ye bought this farm," said Patrick to Carroll.

Carroll shrugged. "That proves nothing. I have plenty of money and several people can testify that I have been looking to expand me breeding business. They'll think nothing of it. In addition, the case is closed in Ireland." He chuckled. "They found Fionn's bones after all."

Murphy stepped forward. "Let's get movin' back to the chateau. I be cold and tired. We'll decide what to do with the two of ye in the morning. In the meantime, I have work yet to do."

With guns at their backs, Patrick and Ronan were shoved toward the chalet. Shaken and afraid, Patrick moved slowly away from the stable . . . away from Fionn.

Chapter 42

Maddie knew the wait would be long and had prepared herself with a blanket, a good book, and a flashlight. But as she sat in the lonely truck, she found it hard to concentrate on what she was reading. She checked her watch frequently. The three friends had estimated the recovery would take an hour or more . . . if all went smoothly. Yet, for Maddie, time seemed to have stopped.

A strange scratching sound from outside the truck made her jump and drop the book and flashlight on the floor. After reaching down to retrieve the book, she sat back up and found herself staring at a dark mass on the hood of her truck.

With shaking hands, she fumbled around until she found the flashlight. Pointing it out the windshield, the white beam rested upon a large raccoon staring back at her. His round eyes glowed with the reflection of the light. Maddie laughed. "You scared me, fella," she said, trying to slow her hammering heart. Pulling her hair back in a ponytail, she scolded herself. "Take it easy Madeline. You are being ridiculous. Everything is fine – just fine." She looked around at the darkness surrounding her and took a deep breath. "Yes – just fine."

She tried to turn her attention back to her book but found it impossible to focus on what she was reading. She sighed with resignation and tossed the book on the passenger seat. Clasping the steering wheel with both hands she looked at her friend, still warming himself on the hood of her truck. She smiled at the odd sense of comfort her new companion gave her. She started singing a favorite song and tapping out the rhythm on the steering wheel. That filled a few minutes, and she checked her watch again.

After checking her watch for perhaps the hundredth time, she was relieved to see that the hour was finally up. She got out of the truck and walked to the back of the horsebox. Unhooking the latches that held the ramp up, she lowered the apparatus to the ground. She stepped up and opened the two upper doors and swung them out to the sides. She unhooked the center panel and swung it to one side, giving Fionn as much room as possible to enter the trailer. *It's amazing that horses trust us enough to put them in one of these dark, tiny boxes,* she thought, shaking her head. And with no daylight, this box was especially dark.

She walked to the front of the trailer to check for the sweet feed and carrots she placed inside the feeder earlier. She knew it was there, but it gave her something to do.

Maddie sat down in the back of the trailer, out of the drizzling rain, and stared into the darkness. She hoped to hear the clip-clop of a horse on the road, but only silence greeted her ears. She turned her flashlight on and pointed it at her watch. She sucked in a deep breath and let it out slowly. It had been well over an hour since the boys left. *Is something wrong?* She wondered. *How long should I wait?*

She stood up and went back to the front of the trailer to check the feed bin again. Of course, nothing had changed. The scoop of grain with the carrots on top was still there. She paced back and forth within the horsebox for several more minutes. Reaching the ramp at the back opening, she stopped and listened. Shielding her eyes, she peered into the darkness and rain. Nothing. Her hands felt clammy, and she rubbed them on her pant legs. Shivering, she pulled the zipper on her jacket up to her neck. She undid her ponytail and replaced it higher up on the back of her head. Then, making up her mind once and for all, she burst out of the horsebox, crossed the road, and plunged into the forest.

Chapter 43

Deciding to reach the lane behind the gate as quickly as possible, Maddie remained close to the road as she struggled through the thick brush and around the dense clusters of trees. Brushing thorny vines away from her face, her hands were soon scratched and bleeding. When she reached the gate, she worked at breaking branches and pulling back vines and brush to clear a passage for Fionn. Then, again staying close to the forest, she rushed down the lane toward the chateau.

Nearing the end of the forest, Maddie was surprised to see yellow beams of light streaming through the trees. Getting closer, she saw lights on in the manor and heard voices coming from outside. She ducked into the thick forest and moved to the edge, concealed in the darkness. Peering around a tree trunk at the edge of a vast lawn she gasped. Her hand flew to her mouth, stifling a cry that wanted to escape from her throat. She watched, stunned, as Patrick and Ronan were being prodded with guns in their backs toward the chateau. The large structure was alive with lights coming from all the main floor windows. The upper floors were dark.

Maddie felt her heart pound and her breath come in short, quick spurts. *Oh, no*, she thought. *What shall I do?* She immediately had her answer. *Get Fionn.*

When the four men entered the chateau, Maddie kept hidden in the shadows as she made her way to a small barn set in the area of the estate from which Patrick and Ronan and the two men had come. The lights in the building were still on. She slid the front door open but a crack, slipped inside, and closed it behind her. She paused as she looked around. There were four stalls, two on either side of the center aisleway.

Straight in front of her at the end of the aisle was a tractor.

"Fionn," Maddie said softly. "Fionn, are you here?"

A bay horse with a dirty white blaze appeared over the second stall door on the left.

Maddie's heart skipped a beat. She smiled and rushed to the stall. Finding his headstall and lead on the ground, she picked them up and entered the stall.

"Hi boy. I've come to help you," she said, weaving her fingers through his black forelock and slipping him a carrot.

Chapter 44

As Maddie was making her way to the stallion barn, Patrick and Ronan were pushed and shoved into the foyer of the stately chateau. Straight ahead, a carved wooden staircase led up to the second floor. The walls were covered with blue and white *Toile de Jouy*, best known as "Toile," patterned linen. The copious woodwork was stained a dark brown. Double French doors stood open on their right, the entrance to a grand living room. The walls in this room were paneled in mahogany. The floor was covered in oriental rugs in deep reds. At the far end of the room, a fire burned in a fireplace set among floor-to-ceiling bookcases and adorned with an ornately carved mantel.

"Get in there, lads," said Carroll.

A man was standing in front of the fireplace, his back to them.

The man by the fireplace turned his tall slender frame around slowly and flashed them a disingenuous smile. Patrick's mouth dropped. It was the man from the bistro.

"Welcome, Patrick and . . ." he paused while looking at Ronan. "Forgive me, I don't know your name."

"This be me friend, Ronan Boyle. But, please forgive *me*, I don't know to whom I be speaking," said Patrick, trying to keep his voice calm.

The man raised his eyebrows. "Don't tell me you don't know the name of the man who has been paying your salary for nearly two years." He turned to Darren Murphy. "I must say, you have done a better job than I expected keeping my identity a secret.

"As instructed, sir," added Murphy, his eyes lowered.

"I appreciate obedience and loyalty in my staff," the man added, the corners of his mouth curling up, taking the goatee with it.

Turning back to Patrick, he said, "My name is Silas El Mari. I am from Dubai, though I spend most of my time traveling."

'Y-you be the owner of Far and Away Farm and Fionn?" Patrick stammered.

"And your boss," El Mari added, a smirk on his face.

Patrick shook his head, and rubbed his hand across his forehead, trying to make sense of this. Here he stood in a room with the man who owned Fionn, another man who enabled the kidnapping of the prize stallion, and still another man who had always wanted to own both the stallion and his home. Now it appeared that the three of them were co-conspirators in this terrible crime.

El Mari stepped up to Patrick and Ronan. "I can see you are confused."

Patrick snorted.

"Dumbstruck, no doubt," said El Mari.

"To put it mildly," said Ronan.

"Please tell us what be going on," said Patrick, forcing himself to square his shoulders, lift his chin, and look the man in the eyes.

"It's quite simple, really," said El Mari. "Money. And lots of it."

"I thought you already had lots of it," said Patrick.

"One can never have enough."

"But why the kidnapping? Fionn would bring in lots of money as a stud."

"So true. But sometimes money is needed immediately. Such is the case here. A forty-million-pound insurance payout is just what I need at the moment," said El Mari, smoothing his luxurious robe with his bejeweled hands.

"But where does Mr. Carroll fit in?" asked Patrick, glancing over at the Irishman who was standing at the other side of the room, pouring himself a glass of the black stuff.

"He was desperate to have the horse. Is that not right, William?"

"That be true," said Carroll. His eyes narrowed and a "G-r-r-r-r" arose from his throat.

"With this plan, we were both to get our wish," said El Mari. "That is until *you* stepped in and messed everything up." The tall, thin man glared at the two boys. "Because of *you*, Fionn will have to be destroyed."

"You wouldn't be that cruel," said Patrick.

"Oh, no?" said El Mari with a faint malevolence in his voice. "Just watch me. All evidence must be destroyed. At this point, the horse is nothing more than evidence." He turned to Murphy. "You know what to do, Darren."

"Yes, sir," said Murphy. He looked at Patrick with sadness in his eyes.

Chapter 45

Six months earlier . . .

The phone on the entry table rang in the Carroll residence in Dublin. The stately home had been in the Carroll family for generations. Once far from the center of town, it was now surrounded by homes and bordered by busy streets. But the high stone walls, covered with vines, gave the Carroll family the security and privacy they demanded.

A butler answered the phone. "Carroll residence. How may I help you?"

"I would like to speak to William Carroll," said the voice on the other end of the line.

"Is he expecting your call?"

"No. I don't need appointments. Just tell him Silas El Mari is on the line. And be quick about it."

The butler didn't appreciate being spoken to in such a manner. He glared at the receiver as he slowly placed it on the table. The name Silas El Mari meant nothing to him. He walked as slowly as possible to find Mr. Carroll. He knew where he would be – in his study as usual, smoking a cigar and reading the racing news.

The butler tapped quietly on the heavy wooden door and waited.

"Come in."

Opening the door slowly, the butler stepped into the room, stifling a cough from the choking smoke. "A call for you, Mr. Carroll."

"Who be disturbing me at this hour?" Carroll said, dropping the newspaper onto the floor beside his wingback chair.

"The caller identified himself as a Mr. Silas El Mari."

Carroll's face immediately turned several shades of red. "What could that foreigner be calling me for? He's already taken everything I want away from me?"

"Would you like me to tell him you are not available?"

Carroll paused and let out a deep breath. "No. I guess me curiosity has the better of me. I'll take the call here in me study. Please shut the door and hang up the other line."

"As you wish, sir," said the butler as he made his exit.

William Carroll pushed himself out of his chair and walked over to his desk, still confused and uncertain about the purpose of the call from the man he considered an enemy. He sat down in his desk chair and picked up the receiver. "William Carroll, here."

"Carroll, I'm sure your man told you it was me who was calling."

"Yes, Mr. El Mari. I can't hide the fact that I be surprised to hear from ye considering our history."

"Yes. Yes. But let's let bygones be bygones. I have called with an interesting business proposition for you."

Carroll drummed his fingers on his desk, not at all sure that he wanted to partner with this snakein-the-grass on any type of venture. But he responded in the positive. "Go on. I be listening."

"As we both know, you want Fionn."

"*Wanted*. I'm beyond that now."

"Are you? What would you say if I said you could have him?"

Carroll took a quick breath and felt his heart leap to his throat. "I'd say 'What be the catch?'"

El Mari chuckled. "It is wise to be cautious."

"There not be a good history between us."

"True, but the stallion has just completed a very successful first year as a stud. Thirty-five mares are now carrying his foals. And there are even more mares lined up for breeding next season."

"I be aware of that. What does that have to do with me?"

"I am willing to see that you get the stallion."

Confused, Carroll dropped his head in his hands. He mumbled into the receiver. "How is this to come about?"

"It is quite complicated, really, but I have most of it figured out." El Mari cleared his throat. "I have just taken out a forty-million-pound life insurance policy on Fionn."

Carroll let out a whistle. "That be a lot of money."

"Yes. And it is money that I am in need of very soon for a new venture I am interested in."

"But ye can't collect the money unless the hearse is . . ." Carroll stopped, shocked at what he was hearing.

"Dead," finished El Mari. "Yes."

"Ye can't be serious."

"About killing the horse? Of course, I don't want to do that . . . unless it is absolutely necessary. That is why I am contacting you."

"What could I possibly do? The hearse be only valuable to me if he be alive."

"Hear me out," said El Mari. "My plan would keep the horse alive, and you would be the beneficiary of all his progeny going forward to improve your own racing stock."

Over the next two hours, Carroll and El Mari hashed out their diabolical plan to negotiate with the IRA to trade arms for the horse. El Mari had contacts in the IRA, as well as arms dealers in the Middle East. Carroll would deal with affairs in Ireland and France.

And, thus, the crime was put in place. And six months later, Fionn's loyal jockey would find himself under armed guard as Fionn was about to be killed.

Chapter 46

Maddie was in Fionn's stall buckling his headstall around his head. Suddenly, she heard the barn door slide open, the metal wheels scraping on the metal track. Her chest tightened; her breath became trapped inside her chest. She quickly removed Fionn's headstall and dropped to the straw, crouching in the corner beneath the water bucket. Whoever came in went into the neighboring stall that held the large chestnut stallion.

Fionn bent down and nuzzled her cheek. She pushed his lovely head away and tried to quiet her breathing.

"Here big boy. I'm moving you to a different stall."

Maddie recognized the voice. Darren Murphy.

Soon, she heard the clip-clop of hooves on the brick aisleway. She rose just far enough to look over the wall of Fionn's stall and watched Murphy lead the horse out into the night. She knitted her brows. *What is he up to?* she wondered.

A few minutes later she heard footsteps again. Murphy had returned. This time he went to the stall across the aisle that held the dapple gray. Maddie crouched down, afraid to move an inch, afraid to even breathe.

She listened as the same thing happened. He clipped on the headstall and led the horse out into the night.

Maddie felt her nerves stand on end. *Would he be coming for Fionn next?* She looked around the barn for a place to hide.

Parked at the end of the aisle, in front of the stacks of hay and straw, was a rather old and rusty tractor. She had noticed it when she first came into the barn but thought nothing of it. Now she viewed it with different eyes.

Maddie left Fionn's stall, closing the stall door, and releasing the headstall on the ground where she had found it a few minutes before. She hurried over to the tractor. Dropping to her hands and knees, she crawled between the large back tires and curled into a ball.

A few jagged breaths later, she heard Murphy return. Her heart pounded in her chest, and she forced herself to take slow, silent breaths. Listening to the location of his footfalls, she realized he was going to the bay stallion's stall across from Fionn. A minute later, he had the horse out of his stall and leading him into the dark of night.

Now, Maddie was sure Fionn would be next, and she curled up tighter behind the large wheel nearest his stall.

But that was not what happened.

When Murphy returned, he went to the stack of straw near the tractor and pulled out a bale. He slid it to the front of the barn. He returned and did the same with another bale, and then another. Maddie watched him from her hiding spot. Her brow was furrowed as she tried to figure out what he was doing.

After lining up the straw bales across the doorway, Murphy turned. His shoulders were slumped, and he sighed dejectedly as he walked to Fionn's stall.

"I be so sorry to have it end this way, Fionn. Ye didn't deserve it." Pulling a carrot out of his pocket he fed it to the stallion, stroked his face, and turned away. For a brief moment, Maddie thought she detected a hint of sorrow on his face. But then it was gone.

What happened next would always be seared in Maddie's memory.

Murphy took a lighter from his pocket and set the straw bales on fire.

Chapter 47

Maddie gasped and her hand flew to her mouth to stifle the scream that wanted to explode from her chest. With eyes wide in horror, she watched Murphy leave the flaming bales and shut the barn door. The flames spread rapidly and soon the bales were all on fire, sending flames into the air and up the inside wall of the barn.

Maddie collapsed back against the tire as she clutched her chest. Tears stung her eyes. Her muscles tightened as she looked from side to side around the barn. She felt disoriented and she struggled to focus on the danger she was in.

Suddenly a flush of adrenaline coursed through her body, and she knew what she needed to do.

Crawling on hands and knees, she got out from under the tractor. Climbing into the metal seat, she searched around for the ignition, hoping it held a key as most farm tractors did. She was in luck. Dangling from the slot, her hand brushed against a horse-head-shaped key chain. The key was inserted snuggly in the ignition.

"Please start, please start," she pleaded as she turned the key. With a cough and a rattle, the engine came to life. Glancing up to heaven she said a quick prayer of thanks before putting the tractor in gear and pushed the throttle up. She raised the loader bucket halfway and took her foot off the brake. The tractor started moving down the aisle toward the flames.

As they reached the bales, she moved the throttle all the way up to increase the speed to maximum and jumped from the tractor, sending it charging through the wall of fire and smashing through the barn door.

She ran to Fionn's stall and put his headstall on his head. Pulling open the stall door, she grabbed a chunk of mane, swung her leg up and over the panicking horse's back, hunched over his neck, buried her face in his mane, and dug her heels in his sides. Fionn let out a loud squeal, tossed his head, and started toward the opening that was framed by flames. Maddie closed her eyes, held her breath, and settled in low for a ride to save both their lives.

Murphy was halfway back to the chateau when he heard the sound of a tractor starting up followed by splintering wood. He spun around in time to see the tractor crash through the barn door. He stood, frozen in place, his mouth agape at the scene before him.

The tractor came to a stop several meters past the rubble. Flames began pouring out of the opening. And through the flames, a horse with a rider on his back burst out of the barn and galloped down the drive.

Murphy stood where he was and smiled.

Chapter 48

By the time the people in the house were aware of the commotion outside, Maddie and Fionn had reached the copper gate that sealed off the estate from the road. Swinging her right leg over Fionn's hindquarters, she dropped to the ground and led the stallion through the curving path she had created in the forest. Pushing vines and branches aside as they wound between the trees, they struggled to get out to the road. Once there, Maddie ran beside Fionn as she trotted him all the way to where the horsebox was sitting in wait. The ramp was down, the divider open, just as she left it.

"Here we are, boy. Walk," she said as she gave a tug on the lead. She led him up to the ramp. Fionn stopped abruptly and raised his head as his white-rimmed eyes scanned the surroundings. He peered through the rain and into the darkness that surrounded them.

"Walk, Fionn," Maddie said as she struggled to catch her breath.

Fionn hesitated for only a moment more before cautiously lifting a front hoof and placing it on the ramp.

"There's a boy," Maddie said. "Keep walking."

The horse followed Maddie into the horsebox even though he was still quivering with both fear and excitement.

Maddie was struggling to calm herself. Her hands trembled as she clipped the tie onto Fionn's headstall, latched the trailer doors, and lifted the ramp.

She had acted without really considering the possible consequences. She was finding it hard to believe she acted in such an uncharacteristically rash manner. But here she was, back at the trailer with Fionn safely tucked inside.

But what of Patrick and Ronan? She hadn't thought of them from the time she saw them being forced into the house until this very moment. She turned back and looked down the road toward the entrance to the chateau. Nothing. No one had followed her, not even the boys. At least not yet.

"I need to get you to a safe place, Fionn," she said through the open window of the trailer. "Then I'll worry about Patrick and Ronan."

Fionn responded with a toss of the head, the stomp of a hoof, and a loud snort. It seemed he was suggesting they hurry.

She climbed into the truck, started the engine, and pulled out onto the road. Only then did she release the breath she had been holding for far too long.

Back at the chateau, Darren Murphy was joined on the lawn by William Carroll, Silas El Mari, Patrick, and Ronan. Murphy was the only one who knew Fionn and an unidentified rider had escaped. And he wasn't telling anyone.

Patrick collapsed to the ground. Tears streamed down his cheeks. "No. Ye evil people.

How could ye do this . . . to that . . . magnificent hearse?" he choked out between sobs.

Ronan kneeled beside him and put an arm over his shoulder. He had nothing he could say that would ease his friend's pain, so he just sat silently, watching the flames consume the barn.

A short time later, Darren Murphy's wife and children, dressed only in their night clothes, ran out of the house and across the lawn to where the men had gathered.

"Darren!" Mrs. Murphy cried. "Oh, Darren! This be terrible. The hearses! What has become o' the hearses?"

"Three of the stallions be safe in the big barn," Murphy said, putting his arm around her shoulders.

"And the fourth?" she asked, the flames reflecting in her moist eyes.

Murphy shook his head but said nothing more.

Mrs. Murphy clutched her hands to her chest. Agony spread across her face. It was only then that she noticed Patrick and Ronan on the lawn in front of her.

"Do me eyes deceive me? Be that Patrick?" she said, rushing forward and dropping to her knees.

Patrick looked up, his eyes cold and dark, his jaw clenched. He let out a deep breath.

"Oh, Patrick. Do tell me that it be not Fionn trapped in that fire."

"Ask yer husband," Patrick snarled.

Mrs. Murphy snapped her head around and glared at Murphy. "What be the lad sayin'?"

Murphy dropped his head.

William Carroll stepped up to her. "Pay him no mind. He be distraught at the loss of his hearse."

Mrs. Murphy jumped to her feet. "He be distraught? And what about the rest of ye? I knew all along there be somethin' amiss in this whole affair." She looked at Carroll, glaring. "I wanted to think that ye offered me husband a new job because ye respected his skills. But when we got here and I discovered Fionn was here . . . well, things just didn't make sense anymore." She whirled and turned on El Mari. "And then *you* appeared. I want to know what this be all about, and I want to know now!"

El Mari folded his arms across his chest. His eyes narrowed and a sneer covered his face. "I don't answer to anyone, especially not a woman."

At that moment sirens were heard coming from the road.

"Oh, ye don't, don't ye?" said Mrs. Murphy, shaking a finger in his face. "Well perhaps ye will answer to the police!"

Chapter 49

While Maddie, Patrick, and Ronan were driving toward the Chateau Dubois outside Saint Quentin earlier in the evening, the mail was being delivered in Ireland. A certain letter addressed to Sir Bran Gallagher was slipped through the brass mail slot in the center of the dark green wooden door of the trainer's residence just down the road from Far and Away Farm. It sat on the area rug placed over the wood floors in the entry for the rest of the afternoon.

Sir Gallagher was late arriving home. He had a meeting with other members of the Irish

Thoroughbred Breeders Association. The topic of discussion was, of course, Fionn. Fear was running rampant among the members. Their concern was for the safety of their own horses as The Troubles in Ireland continued and the IRA grew more powerful. No one wanted to have their horses stolen and held for ransom, or, even worse, found dead in the end.

The discussions centered around having a unified agreement to refuse to pay any ransom and to make this decision known publicly through all newspapers, radio, and television broadcasts.

The one topic that was also discussed, but one that would not be made public, was how to increase security in and around the stables. A representative from a security company spoke about the options available to farm owners and managers while taking advantage of the opportunity to promote his own products.

Gallagher was tired when he finally did get home, too tired to deal with the mail. Intending to do nothing more than set it on the side table, he bent down and picked it up. However, the envelope sitting on top caught his attention. Handwritten on the envelope was not only his name and address but in the upper left corner was printed: "Le Parc Youth Hostel" with the name "Patrick McCallin" scribbled beneath the address in Saint Quentin, France. That was enough for Gallagher to open it on the spot.

Reaching for his reading glasses, he held the letter in the light of the table lamp.

Sir Gallagher,

I want you to know that I have found the real Fionn as I told you over the phone. The horse skeleton that was found in Ireland is not him. He is being held at a farm outside Saint Quentin, France. The farm is named Chateau Dubois. William Carroll is the owner of the farm, so I know he is involved in the kidnapping. And Darren Murphy is working for him. There is another man, who I don't know, that is a part of this as well. Ronan, Maddie, and I are going to attempt a rescue tomorrow night. If you have not heard from me by the time you read this letter, call the police immediately.

Sincerely,
Patrick

Sir Gallagher dropped the letter. It fluttered to the floor. Reaching for the phone on the side table, Fionn's trainer called the international operator and asked for the local police in Saint Quentin.

Chapter 50

Before the sun even had time to prepared itself to rise in the east and cast its rays beneath a bank of clouds, Maddie arrived at Wattrelos where she had secured a stall for Fionn. The ninety-minute drive from Saint Quentin had been a miserable one. Part of the misery was caused by the lashing of the rain. While the windshield wipers pushed away the rain, there was nothing that could push away the tears falling from her eyes and streaming down her cheeks. The reality of the danger she had been in, and her remarkable escape pressed down on her, while fear for Patrick and Ronan filled her heart. It had taken most of an hour for her heart rate to reach anywhere near normalcy.

When she arrived at the barn, she quickly unloaded Fionn and settled him in his stall with fresh water and a few flakes of hay. Then she went up to the farmhouse and banged on the door. She rubbed the back of her neck and rocked back and forth while she waited for someone to answer the door.

The door opened wide, and her friend's father greeted her with a smile. "Mademoiselle Segard! Did you succeed? Did you get the horse?"

"He's in the barn," she said.

Clearly sensing her anxiety, he said, "Then, what's the matter?"

"My friends are still being held there," she said, her voice shaking.

"What do you mean?"

"The men who stole Fionn have captured Patrick and Ronan."

"Then we must call the Gendarmes at once," he said, pulling her inside the house and shutting the door.

Chapter 51

The police arrived at the Chateau Dubois only to find the copper gate securely locked. A sturdy pair of metal cutters made short work of it. After throwing open the gates, the two police cars zoomed up the narrow drive, their sirens blaring and their lights flashing. Their tires tossed gravel to the side as they came to a sudden halt in front of the little group of people standing on the lawn.

Two officers in full uniform exited each of the cars. The largest of the officers approached the group.

"Good evening." Glancing at the burning barn he added, "We've called in the fire department. They should be arriving soon. But we have come on another matter."

William Carroll stepped forward. "Thank ye, officers. We appreciate yer concern. With the firemen on their way, there be no further need of yer help."

"On the contrary, sir. We are here on an entirely different matter," the officer said as his eyes moved over to look at Patrick and Ronan. "We have a report that two young men are being held here against their will."

The policemen escorted Mr. and Mrs. Murphy and their children, William Carroll, Silas El Mari, Patrick, and Ronan into the chateau. Mrs. Murphy hustled her children up the grand staircase before returning.

Patrick should have been relieved that he was being rescued, but all he could think about was Fionn. He was filled with both anger and mourning. His heart ached and his mind was a jumble of thoughts. *How could they do this? Is there any way Fionn could have escaped? No. Not possible.*

For Patrick, it was like losing a best friend.

The officers ushered everyone into the large living room and told them to be seated. All but El Mari complied. He chose to go to the end of the room and stand by the fireplace. Resting his arm on the mantle, he faced the policemen, his face a mask.

An eerie silence filled the room as everyone waited for the officers to speak. Patrick felt a heavy wall of angry tension hanging over them all.

"Who would like to tell me what's going on here?" the largest officer asked.

"Pardon me," Carroll said, his eyes shifting from side to side. "But ye be the ones who barged into me house, treating all of us like we be criminals. Perhaps *ye* should tell *us* what be going on here."

Pent-up rage and frustration boiled over and Patrick leaped to his feet. "Officers," he said pointing to Carroll and El Mari, "these men are responsible for the kidnapping, and now the death, of the Irish racehorse, Fionn." His heart hurt for the friend he had lost. Somehow, saying it out loud made it all real. Taking a deep breath, he continued, "Ma friend Ronan and I discovered the hearse was here at the farm and we came to rescue him."

Ronan jumped up and joined him. "They caught us and captured us at gunpoint. Then they burned the barn and . . ." Ronan dropped his chin to his chest as tears welled up in his eyes.

El Mari stepped away from the fireplace and approached the center of the room. "Officers, officers," he said, his voice condescending as he painted a smile across his face. "I am Silas El Mari, the well-known and respected businessman from Dubai. I am, or *was*, the owner of the said racehorse, Fionn. Sadly, his remains have been found in a shallow grave in Ireland. The Irish Garda have closed the case." He let out a quiet, terrible laugh as the tendons on his neck twitched. "What these boys are telling you is a complete fabrication, a total lie."

Mrs. Murphy, who had been sitting on the edge of the couch next to her husband jumped up. "No! What the boys say be true, every word of it!" She held up her hand, palm out. "I swear on me grandmother's grave I saw the hearse on this very property."

Chapter 52

Patrick and Ronan watched from the front porch of the chateau as Carroll, El Mari, and Mr. Murphy were placed into the backs of the police cars.

The fire trucks had arrived earlier and were still working to put out the fire.

Patrick turned to Ronan. "What has become of Maddie?"

Ronan shrugged his shoulders and shook his head. "The plan was for her to leave if we didn't return with the hearse within two hours. I just assume she be gone. I'm guessing she be the one who alerted the authorities."

"Either she did, or Sir Gallagher did," Patrick added.

Ronan looked at Patrick with raised eyebrows. "Sir Gallagher?"

"Well, I felt we might need a little back-up, so I sent him a letter."

Ronan clapped Patrick on the back. "Ach! Good thinkin', lad. I be mighty glad ye did."

The two young men walked down the lane toward the copper gates. The sun was just beginning to light the eastern sky, but the thick forest kept a tight hold on the darkness. They reached the country road and continued walking to where they left Maddie's little Renault. They were somewhat relieved to find Maddie and the horsebox gone. *At least,* Patrick reasoned, *she be safe.*

A full ninety minutes later, Ronan drove up to Maddie's parents' home in Lille. Parking the car, they hurried to the door. Patrick reached out and pushed the doorbell. Maddie's mother opened the door.

"Oh, boys!" she said as she threw her arms around both of them in a tight hug. "I am so relieved."

Patrick pulled away. "Be Maddie here?"

"No, but worry not, she is safe. She called me from a friend's house in Wattrelos. Her only concern was for you." Madame Segard stepped back. "Forgive me. Please come in. I'll fix you a big breakfast."

Patrick shook his head. *"Buíochas,"* Patrick said, lapsing into Irish Gaelic to thank her. "Be we be more eager to see Maddie and talk to her than we be hungry."

Ronan elbowed him. "Speak for yerself," he said.

"Let me send you with some croissants and directions to Wattrelos," Madame Segard, said while stepping away from the door.

Five minutes later, Ronan was driving the Renault in a northeastern direction toward Wattrelos. They had eaten all the croissants before they passed through Hem.

Patrick was struggling to find a way to tell Maddie about Fionn. "What do I say?" he said, turning to face Ronan.

Ronan bit his lip and shook his head.

"She's going to be devastated," Patrick said.

"No more so than ye be," Ronan said, keeping his eyes on the road.

Patrick dropped his chin and sighed.

As they drove the narrow roads leading to Wattrelos, Patrick rehearsed what he might say, finally deciding to just tell her the truth as quickly as possible. There was no way to soften the blow.

When they pulled into Maddie's friend's home, they were relieved to see the truck and horsebox parked near the barn.

Patrick pushed his tired and reluctant body out of the little car and dragged himself to the house. He suddenly felt the lack of sleep. He waited on the porch for Ronan to join him before knocking.

A balding, middle-aged man in a white button-down shirt and baggy blue jeans answered the door. His look of inquiry immediately changed to one of joy as a broad smile spread across his face. "Maddie," he called over his shoulder. "You have guests."

Maddie squealed and fairly flew out the door, nearly knocking the boys off the porch. Tears burst from her large, brown eyes. "You are safe. You are safe," she repeated over and over.

Patrick and Ronan returned the hugs.

"Until we got here and were ambushed by a crazy French girl," Ronan said.

Maddie giggled and released her hold on them. "I'm sorry. I've just been so worried. Did the Gendarmes rescue you?"

"They did. *Buíochas*," said Patrick. "But Maddie, I be afraid that I have some terrible news for ye."

Maddie lifted her finger and pressed it against Patrick's lips. "Shush. Just follow me." She leaped off the porch and started running to the barn.

Patrick and Ronan looked at one another, their eyebrows raised.

"Well, I guess we best follow the lass," said Ronan.

As they arrived at the little barn set a short distance from the house, Maddie clasped the rusty handle on the weathered door and pulled. The metal wheels at the top, badly in need of oil, screeched in complaint. The wind blew dust and pieces of straw into their faces as they entered the dark barn.

Maddie led the way.

As Patrick's eyes adjusted to the darkness, he noticed several old pieces of farm equipment, a stack of hay in need of straightening, and two stalls constructed of scrap boards attached in a haphazard fashion to the support posts. Then he saw *him*.

In one of the stalls was a large, bay Thoroughbred whose brown coat was covered with black splotches. A dirty white stripe ran down his face.

Chapter 53

Patrick felt his heart go faint and he thought his knees were going to buckle. Bracing himself against the wall of the stall, he breathed out, "Fionn."

Maddie stood at the horse's head and grinned.

"Ok, lass. Ye better start talkin'," Ronan said, his arms folded across his chest and a smile on his face.

"Yes, Maddie. How did ye get him here? We saw the barn in flames."

Maddie blushed. "Well, I hate to brag but I can be pretty remarkable, sometimes." She proceeded to tell them all she had done since they parted ways in front of Chateau Debois, finishing with sending the tractor through the wall of flames and galloping Fionn out of the burning barn.

The two boys stood spellbound by her tale, finding it almost beyond belief.

While Patrick and Fionn were being reunited, Carroll, El Mari, and Murphy were sitting in a musty, cramped cell in the Saint Quentin police headquarters. El Mari continued to demand, in the loudest voice he could muster, to speak to his team of attorneys.

Carroll asked for a warmer blanket and softer pillow.

Murphy sat on his cot, his hands clasped, his head down. The anger boiling inside him was directed primarily at himself. His thoughts tormented him. *How could I have been so stupid? How could I have gone along with this? What's going to become of me family? What's going to become of me?*

The Garda from Newbridge and Sir Gallagher from Far and Away Farm were summoned to Saint Quentin. They arrived late in the afternoon after flying in and landing on a small, private runway to the north of town. Upon their arrival, a large meeting room was made available, and all parties were brought together. The French police intended to get to the bottom of the whole affair.

Sir Gallagher sat in the straight-backed chair, his head down, the veins in his neck twitching, as El Mari and Carroll spun their story. They denied ever stealing Fionn. The horse the "youngsters" assumed was Fionn was simply a horse that looked like him. Carroll's purchase of the Chateau Debois was all on the up and up. Carroll, with El Mari's backing, was merely trying to break into the French racing scene.

Sir Gallagher glanced over at his long-time friend, Darren Murphy. He couldn't help but interpret the look on the man's face as one of both remorse and desperation with a hint of resignation. The man had a great reputation as an outstanding stable manager, but more importantly as a fine father and husband. All of that was at risk of being taken from him. *Perhaps*, Sir Gallager thought, *by his own doing.*

A knock on the door stopped the yarn Carroll was spinning.

"Enter," called out the magistrate.

Two men dressed in firemen's gear walked in carrying a gas can.

At the sight of the can, Murphy broke down in tears, his shoulders shaking, audible sobs escaping his throat.

Darren Murphy's confession put an end to the entire investigation. There was no further need for comment from the Garda or Sir Gallagher.

The charges ranged from kidnapping to insurance fraud, and several things in between.

Chapter 54

Fionn's welcome-home parade was even more grand and exciting than the first when he returned to Ireland and Far and Away Farm after his remarkable racing career was ended. It seemed everyone wanted to see the horse that had come back from the dead. The hero had returned to life, and in some small way, it restored hope to a beaten-down people.

Patrick, Ronan, and Maddie walked beside the beautiful prancing horse as they worked their way past the cheering crowds of people waving green, white, and orange Irish flags. Colorful banners decorated the buildings lining the streets of Newbridge.

"Fionn! Fionn!" the people called out. Shredded colored paper was tossed in the air, making a carpet on which Fionn daintily stepped.

A raised platform had been erected in front of City Hall. It was there the parade ended. The citizens gathered 'round.

"Whoa, boy," Patrick said to Fionn and gave a gentle tug on the lead. Fionn obediently stopped, his head up, his ears twitching as he looked from side to side.

Patrick turned his attention to the platform and noticed that several dignitaries were seated on the stand. He recognized the mayor and the superintendent of the Garda. At the far end, he saw Sir Gallagher. The trainer's face was beaming.

Beside Sir Gallagher, Patrick saw his mother and grandfather. Catherine McCallin was looking at him and smiling, her eyes sparkling. Patrick lifted his hand and offered a slight wave in recognition. His thoughts went to his father, and he wondered if he was proud of him.

There were several other men on the platform whom he did not recognize.

Several journalists snapped pictures while Patrick, Ronan, and Maddie stood expectantly in front of the raised dais.

The mayor arose, stepped to the podium, and welcomed everyone, especially their guests of honor: Patrick McCallin, Ronan Boyle, Madeline Segard, and, of course, Fionn.

"These three young people be heroes," he said. "Because of their bravery, Fionn has returned to us."

A cheer went up from the crowd and more confetti was thrown into the air and fluttered on the breeze.

The mayor let the cheering go on for several minutes before he raised his hands to quiet the crowd. "Yes. We all be excited about the rescue of our beloved hero, Fionn," he said, smiling down at the horse. "But words of thanks are simply not enough. There are some esteemed guests on the stand with me. They have some important announcements ta make." The mayor motioned to the man he had been sitting beside. The man came to the microphone.

"Ladies and Gentlemen," he began, "I am Sir Michael Dunne. I am the current president of the

Irish Thoroughbred Breeders Association. I have joined in your celebration today to make a very important announcement." He paused and looked over the hushed crowd. He smiled. "Fionn's previous owner forfeited his rights to Fionn when he filed for and collected an insurance claim on the horse. This makes Fionn an orphan of sorts," he said with a chuckle that was answered in kind by the crowd.

Patrick, on the other hand, pursed his lips and cocked his head to one side. He could not imagine where this was going. A stab of fear pierced his heart.

"Let me continue," Sir Dunne said. "The Irish Thoroughbred Breeders Association is always striving to improve the breed but also to expand our influence in the horse racing world far and wide. Fionn is an important part of fulfilling that goal. As a result, it is our desire that Fionn stay here, where he belongs . . ." This was met with a loud cheer from the crowd and a snort from Fionn.

Sir Dunne smiled and nodded, then raised his hand for silence. He pulled a folded paper from his pocket and opened it. "The Association has worked with the insurance company to purchase Fionn." Turning the paper toward the audience, he said:

"The name of the new owner, verified on this paper, is Mr. Patrick McCallin of Newbridge, County Kildare, Ireland."

Maddie and Ronan grabbed Patrick from either side to keep him from collapsing.

Mrs. McCallin jumped to her feet and clutched her hands to her chest as a tear coursed down her cheek.

Sir Gallagher raised a fist in the air.

The entire town sent up a collective cheer. Their hometown boys would be together forever.

Author Notes:

ate at night on February 8, 1983, a famous Irish Thoroughbred racehorse named Shergar was kidnapped from the Ballymany stud in County Kildare, Ireland. A gang of armed men drove onto the stud, located next to The Curragh Racecourse, and took The Epsom Derby winner from his stall. They loaded him in a horse trailer and disappeared into the foggy night. A ransom demand of two million pounds was never paid and neither the horse nor his remains were ever found.

To this day, the kidnapping of Shergar has not been solved. Who took him or why remains a mystery, though many theories abound.

"Finding Fionn" is a crime story inspired by this horrific and tragic cold case, but with an ending that I, as a horse-lover, wish had happened.

M.J. Evans

ACKNOWLEDGMENTS

My thanks to Mr. Denny Dressman who not only worked so hard editing but kept me going every time I complained that I didn't know how to write a mystery!

I am also grateful to Mahaut Segard for being my "French Expert."

My deep appreciation to Melanie Heise who helped with the Irish dialogue.

ABOUT THE AUTHOR

M.J. Evans is the author of more than twenty award-winning books for middle-graders, young adults, adults, and even a few picture books. Most of her titles are about horses or horse fantasy creatures. Ms. Evans is a graduate of Oregon State University and a former teacher of middle-school and high school students. She is the mother of five and the grandmother of twelve. She and her husband live in Colorado.

If you enjoyed this book, please take a minute to post a short review on Amazon. That helps others find the book as well.

You can contact M.J. Evans on her website: www.dancinghorsepress.com She loves to receive letters and she always writes back!

Follow her on social media:

Goodreads: https://www.goodreads.com/author/show/4496514.M_J_Evans

Bookbub: https://www.bookbub.com/profile/m-j-evans

Amazon: https://www.amazon.com/M.-J.-Evans/e/B004GM_S014

Instagram: https://www.instagram.com/mjevansbooks

Facebook: https://www.facebook.com/margi.evans.98

Join her email list for *very* occasional updates on new releases and receive a FREE PDF of a short Christmas story. Email her at mjevansbtm@gmail.com and put "Join email list" in the subject line.

ABOUT THE ARTIST

Cover art: "In the Fray" Oil on canvas
by Kamron Coleman

Visit his website to see more of his fabulous
work: www.kamroncoleman.store

Read more Award-Winning Titles by M.J. Evans:

Novels:
The Stallion and His Peculiar Boy
In the Heart of a Mustang
The Sand Pounder
PINTO!
North Mystic
Mr. Figgletoes' Toy Emporium
Series:
The Mist Trilogy-
Behind the Mist
Mists of Darkness
The Rising Mist
The Centaur Chronicles-
The Stone of Mercy
The Stone of Courage
The Stone of Integrity
The Stone of Wisdom
Picture Books:
Percy-The Racehorse Who Didn't Like to Run
The Skullington Family Series-
Boney Fingers
Bone Appetit
School is a Grave Mistake
Skeletons in the Closet

All titles available on the website: dancinghorsepress.com

www.ingramcontent.com/pod-product-compliance
Lightning Source LLC
Chambersburg PA
CBHW072054190726
48294CB00005B/1501